The Devil Duke Takes a Bride

by
Rachel Van Dyken

The Devil Duke Takes a Bride
by Rachel Van Dyken
Published by Astraea Press
www.astraeapress.com

This is a work of fiction. Names, places, characters, and events are fictitious in every regard. Any similarities to actual events and persons, living or dead, are purely coincidental. Any trademarks, service marks, product names, or named features are assumed to be the property of their respective owners, and are used only for reference. There is no implied endorsement if any of these terms are used. Except for review purposes, the reproduction of this book in whole or part, electronically or mechanically, constitutes a copyright violation.

THE DEVIL DUKE TAKES A BRIDE
Copyright © 2012 RACHEL VAN DYKEN
ISBN 13 978-1480214682
ISBN 148021468X
Cover Art Designed by AM Design Studios

This one is for all my readers who have stuck with me since the first regency in the Renwick House Series, The Ugly Duckling Debutante. I hated to let that series go and after many conversations over Facebook, Starbucks, and Twitter, all of you inspired me to write another story based on those characters I loved so much! Thank you so much for your kind words, inspiration, and support! It's been great meeting all of you at conferences and book signings. I would not be where I am today without you! I love you all from the bottom of my heart, thank you for making my job the best job in the world.
☺ Enjoy!

Chapter One

An Unfortunate Turn of Events

Cough, cough, cough. "So, you see, my boy, there isn't another option. I am at the end of my life and in need of this final boon in order to pass into the land of our ancestors."

Benedict Devlyn, Duke of Banbury, was determined not to roll his eyes as he squinted at his more-than-healthy aunt. "Forgive me, but I highly doubt the sniffles will be the death of you. Unless you have some other sort of illness that has you spouting off nonsensical death wishes. Oh wait, yes, did your dog bite you? And it's become infected? Yes, must be it. That's why you're dying, certainly not from sitting too near Lady Renwick when she was ill last week."

"Impetuous man, look at me!"

He *was* looking at her. And all he saw was a woman at the prime old age of one and seventy, with the uncanny ability to hug a man so tightly he nearly lost his countenance. Well, that and he had the sneaking suspicion that for one reason or another, she was lying through her teeth. For his aunt, of all people, to summon him wasn't normal. Nor was answering her every beck and call something he made a habit of doing.

For one thing, it was common knowledge that she was slightly mad, and the other complication was that he and his aunt hadn't been on speaking terms since last season when he decided he would *not* take her dog to Almacks—to her great disappointment. She'd been feigning death ever since.

Her coughing brought him back to the present. Peculiar that it was now changing to a more drastic coughing fit than before. "Is that all then? You wish for me to go find a girl and be done with this whole Devil Duke business?"

"Before I die!" Aunt Agatha interrupted, thrusting her hand into the air. "You are a stain upon the family name."

The witch didn't mince words, did she?

"I see," he said, though truthfully he didn't see. After all, his reputation had been legendary. Every young buck wanted to be him, and every high-stepping mama who threw her debutante his way was given ruin and disaster in return. After ten years of his infamous exploits, women not only gave him the cut direct, but he had it on good authority they now placed his name next to *devil* on all of the finishing school lists when warning debutantes against ruin. In his mind, it was an accomplishment of gigantic proportions.

She trained a cold glare on him, momentarily giving Benedict pause. "Is that it then? You will never marry, even if it's my dying wish? And you plan to enjoy the short years you have left living a life that even the devil himself wouldn't approve?"

Truly it wasn't as bad as all that. She was given to exaggeration. If he *was* that bad, well, he wouldn't be accepted into Society.

And he was accepted everywhere.

He lifted his eyebrows as if waiting for her to continue speaking. When she didn't, he said, "Well, as you can see, I am firm in my belief that I will not change. Good day." He made a move to leave.

She coughed and held up her hand.

Patience was not one of Benedict's virtues, nor was being used by any sort of woman, especially one who still held a grudge the size of London. Devil take it, a blasted dog at Almacks? To see him married before she died? Clearly his aunt was mad, perhaps they had room in Bedlam for one more...

"I truly am dying." Agatha held a trembling hand to her face and winced.

"Ah yes, forgive me for forgetting that minor detail." He took a seat opposite her and waited.

"Hmmph." Agatha crossed her arms and coughed again. "I need to see you settled down before I die, Benedict. My acceptance into heaven depends on it."

That, he believed.

"And what will you give me in return for my obedience? After all, who knows what kind of notion you're bound to get, considering you've been cooped up in your bed all day with the ague. What's to say you won't demand I suddenly begin sprouting children all over the place? Or take up dog-breeding? Or, heaven forbid, offer a smile?"

Aunt Agatha had the good sense to blush before answering. "Believe me, Benedict, finding a bride may prove more difficult than you realize. The idea that you think this to be easy is quite laughable, if I do say so myself." *Cough.*

Laughable? Truly? Biting back a curse, he turned around and ran his fingers through his hair. Mad, his aunt was truly mad. Either that or she had a death wish. How was it that his aunt had the nerve to insult him when the rest of the *ton* was so deathly afraid of him and his reputation that he was rumored to be the spawn of Satan himself?

Not that it kept any sort of married female away from him. Laughable? His aunt didn't know what she was talking about. Perhaps she was truly dying, for the day a woman had the audacity to say no to the Devil Duke would also be the day he would promptly eat his shirt and buy a lap dog.

"And I've already done all the work for you, my boy!"

Why was he not surprised? She probably had a special license underneath that dratted chair she was sitting in, as well.

"And who is to be the victim, Aunt?"

Did her eyes just twinkle? Impossible! The woman was seldom amused. "Lady Katherine Bourne. I do believe you are acquainted, though I also have another female in mind, considering Lady Katherine is a little high in the instep for you, my boy, but not so much for another young fellow I know."

If he would have had a drink in his hand this would have been the opportune moment for him to throw back the remaining contents or slam it against the floor. As it was, he was having a devil of a time keeping himself from cursing in the presence of his aunt, even though one could hardly call her a lady with the way she threw around French expletives.

"You truly mean for me to align myself with that, that..." Obviously his mind was having trouble conjuring up an adequate word to describe the girl in question. So much, in fact, that he could only concentrate on the simple idea that his aunt wanted him in the same room as the chit.

"She's lovely," his aunt pointed out. "And need I remind you that she's a Kerrington? Why, every young man within the city wants to be with the Kerrington family; they are, after all, closely related to the regent himself, and I'm not one to brag—"

Benedict stopped listening when the word *lovely* was mentioned. It seemed this would be the opportune time to remind his aunt of her need for an heir, or at least nieces and nephews to dote on. It certainly would not take place with the

Bourne chit!

"Absolutely not," he interrupted, or at least he hoped he was. Nothing made him happier than interrupting his aunt when she spoke.

Her eyes narrowed. "I don't understand."

Typical, the word *no* wasn't in her vocabulary.

"I mean," Benedict sent up a silent prayer for strength, "That I wouldn't marry the chit if you offered me all the money in the world!"

"She's beautiful!"

"She's as clumsy as she is mad!" Benedict roared.

His aunt squinted and tossed her head from right to left, most likely trying to give him the impression she didn't agree, though it seemed that she was closer to having an apoplectic fit than arguing.

"I disagree." She lifted her chin in the air and sniffed. "You have no proof she did those dreadful things. After all, it has been three years since you've seen her! She's a girl of three and twenty now! Nearly on the shelf."

"I wonder why," he muttered under his breath.

"Oh posh, how much harm could she have done?"

"Harm?" Benedict repeated. "Harm?"

"You said that."

"Harm," he said again, mainly to provoke his aunt. At her scowl, he continued, "She nearly killed me—"

"Truly you exaggerate."

It was obviously time for a drink; Benedict walked to the sideboard and poured three fingers of brandy. "I hardly exaggerate the story. Need I remind you there were witnesses? The girl followed me home. Hid, Aunt! Hid in the bushes and nearly scared my horse out of its wits, tossing me from its back! I was bedridden for a week!"

"Silly accident." His aunt waved it away.

"On our second meeting," he continued, gaining more

courage to argue from the amber liquid swirling in his belly, "she decided to race Lord Rawlings through the fields of the estate and nearly fell of her horse! I had to rescue her, naturally, because Rawlings had so obviously bested her, and when I came upon the fair damsel, she told me to stop, and at that precise moment, I was hit in the face with a tree branch!"

"Again, I'm sure it wasn't on purpose."

Benedict growled low in his throat. "Bedridden, again, three days. Need I go on?"

"Oh, please do." Aunt Agatha sipped her tea. "I do love to hear of your exaggerations. It's as if someone is telling me a bedtime story."

Benedict held up his finger and pointed at his aunt. "The third and final time I was in that girl's presence, and notice I say girl because to call her a woman would be an insult to the sex, I offered to dance with her. Wanted to bury the hatchet and all that. We danced, she was amiable, and then she looked faint. I, being the gentleman that I am..." Aunt Agatha coughed. Saucy wench. "Took her to the outside air. Upon reaching the balcony she leaned over and dropped her reticule. I leaned down to fetch it and managed to topple over onto the ground. Somehow hitting my head a third time. Truly, I'm lucky to be alive."

"Aren't we all so thankful that you are," Aunt Agatha said dryly.

"I won't do it." He poured some more brandy and repeated that same sentiment over and over again.

And when he left, his head ached something fierce. Even the girl was plaguing him from afar. He wouldn't do it. Couldn't do it. He would simply have to find someone else. And fast, for his aunt had something up her sleeve this Christmas, and he wasn't all that sure he wanted to be caught with his drawers down.

****

Benedict approached the following night's ball with as much enthusiasm as a criminal facing the hangman's noose. At this point, he would have welcomed such an end.

He wore his ducal frown, and managed to get in a few distinct growls at his footman before he made his way up the marble steps into The Duke of Montmouth's townhouse.

It was to be the first ball hosted by the duke and his bride, and although it was a time of merriment, all Benedict could truly think of was the fact that the word *merriment* began with *merry*, which of course reminded him of being married, which then made his head hurt, and for some odd reason gave him the distinct impression that he was about to be injured for the fourth time.

Benedict made his way directly to the whiskey and poured himself a healthy glass, not turning to his right or left to make conversation. His sole focus was on the dry liquid as it poured down his throat. It was his job to be scandalous. He knew drinking so early in the evening would be frowned upon, but he didn't give a whit about anything except forgetting he had to participate in the night's festivities.

"That bad?" a male voice said next to him.

"Rawlings?" Benedict could hardly believe his eyes. The once-rakish Lord Rawlings was said to be in the country with his wife. "What the devil are you doing here?"

"Oh, a favor. It seems one of our mutual friends is to be in Town, and my wife hadn't the heart to say no to showing some interest in the girl and showing her about at the parties."

"Ah." Benedict gave a quick smile. "Thus she is floating around the social circles, and you're next to the whiskey?"

"Did I mention that the girl is not but sixteen? And has the distinct pitch of a lap dog getting hit by a carriage?"

Benedict let out a hearty laugh. "Then cheers, old friend."

"Old friend?" The Duke of Tempest approached with a cheery smile on his face. "Just what are we toasting to, and who's trying to steal my friends away?"

Benedict gave a short bow. "Benedict Devlyn, Duke of Banbury."

Tempest laughed, his eyes twinkling. "That sounds about right. What brings you into Town, Devil Duke? I haven't seen you about this Season."

"He avoids it," another male voice cut in.

Truly it was as if the entire male sex could sense that Benedict needed support and were now coming to his aid in throngs.

"Lord Renwick, a pleasure," Benedict said.

"You wouldn't be saying that if you knew who my wife was talking to at this very moment."

"Please do not finish telling me that story if it has anything to do with my—"

"Lovely aunt?" Renwick finished. "Perhaps I overdid it when I said 'lovely'. I'm sure we can conjure up a few more words to adequately describe the—"

"Chit?" Tempest offered.

"Meddlesome bag?" Rawlings input was quite useful.

"Incorrigible, quick witted, opinionated piece of…" Benedict stopped himself when his eyes set on the vision in front of him.

A beautiful woman walked into the room. Her profile was perfect, as if an artist had conjured her from heaven. Her lips, though he could only see the sides, were plump and a pale pink. Golden hair cascaded loosely around her shoulders, falling out of her messily placed bun. And her silver dress wrapped around her perfect form as if it was sewn onto her.

As if his mind had communicated with hers, she turned and looked at him. His stomach dropped, as did his whiskey. He cursed in every language he knew, not caring that the men around him probably thought he caught some sort of madness from his aunt. But he knew, even as she walked toward him and his stomach clenched, and his head pounded like the devil...This was the very same "girl," who had nearly stolen his life three times. The only question hanging in the air between them was whether or not he'd leave this party dead or alive...

Chapter Two

A Matter of Honor

Katherine glanced at the Devil Duke. His face was a combination of smooth planes and perfect form. A muscle twitched in his jaw when he set his eyes on her, and for a minute they darkened, causing her to feel like a nervous girl still in pigtails. And then his once smoldering face turned to something much more predatory. Nostrils flared, fingers clenched at his sides, and then he raised his hand to touch the back of his head as if it ached.

Taking a steadying breath, she straightened her shoulders and made her way toward the man. An apology was surely in order after three years. After all, it hadn't been her fault that he had suffered so much trauma at her hands, he just seemed to have the worst timing and balance out of any man she knew! The man was a walking scandal, sin incarnate. She only hoped she wouldn't be ruined by merely associating with him, for his reputation with debutantes was clearly marked with scandal. Lucky for her, she wasn't some debutante, but practically on the shelf, an old woman. Surely he wouldn't find her the least bit attractive, and if he did? Well, if he did, she would simply have to ignore his virility and handsome face. Perhaps if she closed her eyes she could forget his handsomeness. She tried it.

Of course it did nothing but make her more curious if her mind had conjured up the same image she had just gazed upon.

It hadn't.

He was far more attractive than a man of his reputation should be. She straightened her shoulders and shook the foreboding thoughts from her head.

Regardless of his reputation, she needed to at least acknowledge that all those silly incidents were her fault and her fault alone. Especially if she was to catch the eye of the duke's cousin, whom she knew would be in attendance this very night.

The Dowager Duchess of Durbin had said as much in her letter. And Katherine was thrilled that she would finally get her chance with the Scottish duke. The only man standing in her way was the Devil Duke himself, and she wasn't about to let the obviously negative man get in the way of her happy future.

She swallowed and gave a quick curtsy, slowly raising her eyes toward him and waited. It was most improper for her to even use his last name instead of his title, but to her, the name fit. His last name of Devlyn described him quite perfectly for he was most assuredly descended from the devil himself. Dark hair, dark eyes, wide unforgiving lips, and a sneer fit for a true aristocrat. His eyebrows furrowed as a mocking smile danced across his face.

"Lady Katherine, it has been too long." If she was a betting woman, which she most assuredly was not, she half expected him to continue in that same sentiment, adding that it had not been long enough. Banbury bent over her hand and bestowed a kiss upon it.

Quickly, she tugged it away and rubbed the spot where his lips had touched. Perhaps she was catching a chill? That was why her hand was still shaking when she placed it back at her side. Or maybe she really was frightened of the man.

"Yes, yes it has." Katherine sighed. "I was wondering, if it would not be too bold to ask, your grace, might we take a turn about the room?"

He grimaced. Lovely. Always nice to know a gentleman enjoyed her company. "I believe that would be acceptable." He turned slightly to the left and nodded to the men behind them. Each one of them was a beautiful male specimen, and oddly, looked slightly foxed. She shrugged and took his arm when he offered.

Heavens, her heart was beating out of her chest. Apologies did not come easy to Katherine, and an apology to such a menacing man, even if he did deserve it, was on the bottom of her list.

Banbury paused, allowing a couple to walk by in front of them, and when he did, his other hand reached out and lightly touched her arm as a warning to stop. It should not have meant anything, in fact, he was probably just worried she would somehow cause him to trip and hit his head for the fourth time. Instead, a shiver ran up and down the length of her body, and her heart seemed to take flight as if she were ready to faint.

Truly, the man was so fearsome even her heart was growing weary. They continued toward the back of the room where less people crowded around, and finally she opened her mouth to speak.

"I have something that needs to be said."

"Then say it." His voice was smooth and held no anger, merely impatience.

"I must apologize for any bodily or mental harm I may have caused you in the past. Please accept my sincerest regrets that I have been the cause of so much pain."

Banbury's lips moved into what could possibly be a smile and he brought his hand up to the back of his head. Did he have a headache?

"Do you have any further plans to cause me physical harm, my lady?"

"Not that I am aware of, no."

"Well, just in case, I'll be sure to give you a wide berth when we dance. Now, shall we?" He held out his gloved hand and winked.

Warmth pooled in her belly as she took his hand and joined him in a dance. Truthfully that could not have gone any better! Well, other than the fact that there was a resounding gasp when she allowed him to take her onto the dance floor.

But she paid the onlookers no heed. Now all she needed to do was inquire about his cousin. He turned her around and faced her again.

"Do you often travel to your cousin's estate in Scotland?" she asked.

Banbury narrowed his eyes. "I cannot say that I do. I much prefer my estate near Bath. Though I'm sure my cousin wouldn't be against a familial visit come this spring."

Lost in thought, she merely nodded. Heavens, she hadn't remembered him being so boring or dry. Thankfully she wasn't going to have to be leg-shackled to the man for the rest of her life. Suddenly, she felt quite sorry for the poor miserable woman who would have to share his bed every night. Granted, he was a beautiful male specimen to gaze upon, but looks could only take one so far if he had no sense of humor to speak of and didn't know how to smile if his life depended on it.

As the song ended, her foot caught and twisted in the

bottom of her skirt, sending her reeling into the duke's arms, but she was in so much pain and so mortified, she could only whimper as he helped her off the dance floor and out into the cool night air of the balcony.

"Where does it hurt?" he asked gently, kneeling down at her foot.

Unfortunately she lost her balance and kicked her injured foot into the air trying to regain it, landing a very hard blow to the duke's head.

He let out a curse and fell backward onto the ground with a thud.

"Oh my! Heavens, are you all right?" Momentarily forgetting about her injury, Katherine tried to walk on her bad ankle toward the duke but lost her footing, landing on top of him with her skirts up past her knees. The only reason she knew this was because cold air bit at her calves.

"Get off!" Banbury bellowed.

"I'm trying!" she argued, pushing away from him, but it was nearly impossible to skitter away when his arms were flailing about.

And then all pandemonium broke loose. A gasp was heard from the doorway followed by a cry, and then applause.

The Dowager Duchess of Durbin was sniffing and holding a handkerchief to her eye as if she was shedding tears over their obviously compromising situation. And the three men she had seen earlier drinking with Banbury were now grinning ear to ear, all of them clapping their hands as if they had just witnessed a comedy of errors.

"This isn't what it looks like!" she wailed, peeling herself from the duke's body and accidently kneeing him in the shin as she made her way back to her feet.

The duke didn't speak, nor did he yell. Instead, he closed his eyes and began mumbling things under his breath.

"Is he praying?" the dowager asked.

A blond-headed fellow piped up. "Most likely to be struck by lightning."

"Sounds familiar," a man she now recognized as Lord Rawlings with dark features and crystal blue eyes said, looking quite amused. She hadn't seen him in years, but he still held that rakish air.

She hadn't a clue as to the identity of the other men, mainly because she had been in the country for so long. Assuming they were friends, she felt even more embarrassed that they had all just witnessed such a catastrophic event.

"So," a tall gentleman who hadn't spoken yet said, "When is the wedding to take place?"

Rawlings laughed. "I think he's still praying God will strike him where he lies. Doesn't work that way, fellow. Believe me, I've tried. Now, Renwick, Tempest, let us leave the Devil to his evil doings and have a drink on his behalf. It seems he'll need it."

Katherine wasn't so sheltered that she didn't now understand who the men where. Lord Renwick? The Duke of Tempest? And Lord Rawlings? Two of the most notorious rakes of the *ton* and the Angel Duke himself.

Well, it seemed there was no escaping matrimony. But by George, she was going to try.

Chapter Three

Down for the Count

Perhaps he could merely pretend to have had an apoplexy? How long, he wondered, could a person hold his breath before he did permanent damage to his body? Perhaps if he passed out, he could make up a story about how the woman, who he would now refer to as Eve, tricked him, tripped him, and clobbered him over the head.

He kept his eyes closed just in case his ridiculous plan would work.

It didn't.

Another throat cleared. He stopped his prayers and opened one eye, then two. His aunt's icy blue stare seemed to penetrate his body with such irritation that his head began to hurt again, or was the throbbing merely a happy coincidence with getting hit by Lady Katherine? Saints alive, she was going to be the death of him.

"Look what you've done." Aunt Agatha shook her head and sniffled. Well, at least she was over her imaginary head cold, now it seemed she had nothing but tears and outrage.

"I did nothing wrong, I merely fell after being struck by a blunt object. You cannot fault me in the matter!"

"You compromised that woman! What the devil is wrong with you! Have I not raised you to at least woo a woman before you lift her skirts! Heavens, we are in public!"

"I was accosted!" he yelled.

"You were seducing her!"

"I was unconscious!" He blinked his eyes and cursed. Pain was now throbbing at his temples. Truly, if God were to call him home, he wouldn't fault Him one bit. He'd merely lift his arms heavenward and thank the Lord for taking him. Then again his thanks would be twofold, for he would be grateful to even be near the pearly gates, let alone given free entry.

Aunt Agatha sighed. "Either way, it was bad form, Benedict. Truly bad form. I shall announce your impending marriage at once. Now run along and have yourself some brandy, you look awful. Hmph." With swift movements, she left him on the cold ground, alone and upset. One thing was for certain, he wasn't going to marry the girl. He would rather jump into the Thames in the dead of winter! Although, on second thought, jumping into the Thames would mean he would die of a head injury, considering it was frozen over. Perhaps he could cut out a little hole and jump into it. Sadly, the smile on his face was entirely brought on by his suicide plan, an unfortunate circumstance that. Was marriage truly that ghastly to him?

The woman was a plague, a disease he could not rid himself of! It mattered not that she was beautiful, or that she had grown into those luscious lips and curves. She was still the devil's own to deal with. And he would not align himself with such a lady for the rest of his life. Imagine! Lady Katherine? A Duchess? Married to the Devil Duke himself?

He pushed away from the ground and examined his body

for dirt and smudges. Satisfied, he cracked his neck and walked back into the ballroom. A resounding hush fell upon the people dancing and then the whispering commenced. It was the first time in his existence that people had dared talk about him. Most were too afraid to even utter his name, not that he was a rake of any kind. No, he was merely frightening for most women to talk to. He was dark and brooding and according to the debutantes, fiercely handsome. Rumor was that he would most likely marry a woman and kill her in the bedroom with all of the force of his evil presence.

He let out a long sigh and walked in the general direction of Lord Rawlings, but was intercepted by Lady Katherine herself.

Chapter Four

Innocent as the Driven Snow

"How dare you!" Katherine pointed a shaking finger at the duke, biting back a curse. "I cannot marry you!"

"Finally, something we agree upon," he countered, then looked around them. Muttering a curse, he grabbed ahold of her arm and tugged her toward the back corner of the room where they were given more privacy. "Did you think to trick me into marrying you? Was that it?"

Katherine burst out laughing. Banbury did not seem pleased, his eyebrows furrowed. Looking quite offended, he crossed his arms and scowled. "I assure you, I am quite the catch."

"I'll just have to take your word for it, now won't I? Regardless, you've ruined everything and now your cousin won't even give me—"

"My cousin?" he interrupted. "What about my cousin? Don't tell me you hold a secret tender for the Scottish duke."

Katherine felt her cheeks heat.

"Oh, so *he* is the object of your affection. I would say he was lucky, but it's painfully obvious that luck is never on your side, nor would he be lucky to be chained to you the rest of his days. Imagine the scars he would receive, the bloody noses, the black eyes. Gads, it would look like he boxed at Jackson's every day!"

"That is quite enough!" She pointed a gloved finger at his face and poked him in the chest with her hand. "He is sweet, and kind, and doesn't scowl. At least he knows how to smile!"

"I blasted well know how to smile." Banbury winced.

"Were you trying just now?" she asked sweetly.

His answer was to curse and run a gloved hand through his dark locks. "We cannot allow this to happen. You must cry off."

"Me?" Katherine tightened her hands into fists, but Banbury quickly pulled her aside, shielding her from whomever just passed by. Quickly, he pushed her away, as if she were diseased.

"I cannot simply cry off," she whispered, her voice wavering with emotion. "I would be ruined! Who would want me?"

Banbury rolled his eyes. "It isn't as if you're the belle of the ball currently, is it? What does it matter if you simply cry off? Tell everyone I scared you, that I barked or growled, or simply glared and you fell to your knees in horrified hysterics?"

"Yes, because you're simply terrifying when you're unconscious."

"Apparently it's the only way you can get me on my back, now isn't it?" His hot breath fanned her neck as he stepped closer. Instinctively she moved in, undeterred. "Oh believe me, Banbury. If I wanted you on your back I could get you on your back without any sort of violence." What the devil was she saying? Was she carrying on a flirtation with the Devil Duke? And to say such things aloud! But he was so provoking!

His eyes took on a lazy look as they appeared to darken and almost close completely. And then, he smiled. All white teeth and dimples on either side of his face. Katherine felt her face heat even more as her eyes widened to take in the male beauty in front of her.

"Are you quite sure?"

"Positive." Clenching her teeth, she nearly touched his lips when she breathed out the word. Never would she back down from such a ridiculous man.

His amusement faded as he grabbed her arm and pulled her flush against his body. "Then I would have to say I agree." His lips curved into a devilish smile as they tentatively touched hers. It was a question of a kiss, almost as if he was shocked he was participating. And then as their breaths mingled, he groaned and his lips pushed against hers, molded across her mouth. Need shot through her.

This was how girls were ruined.

This was what her instructors had warned her about.

Dark corners, virile smelling men, and the wet heat of a scorching kiss.

Not knowing what else to do, she held on to the lapels of his coat, but it forced her to lean completely into him. Banbury's arms came around her, his hands slowly moved down her back. With a gasp she prepared to scold him, but the hot invasion of his tongue made her lose all thought. It was wicked and delicious. He groaned and she, in purely unladylike behavior, pushed him further into the alcove against the wall.

"I, ahem, do hope I'm not interrupting anything," a clearly masculine voice said from behind them. With a shriek, Katherine pulled away. Banbury was smiling from ear to ear, his breathing ragged as his dilated eyes looked up. Cursing, he pushed Katherine behind him.

"When did you arrive?"

Katherine lifted her eyes, her stomach dropped at the same time. In horror, she looked into the eyes of the same man she had minutes ago told Banbury she had set her cap for. With a sob, she ran off, away from Devil himself and the man she hoped to marry.

****

"Classic." Baldwyn Sinclair, Duke of Paisley, shook his head at Benedict and burst out laughing. "Tell me, was your plan simply to assault her in order to win her favor or had you not fully thought through your attack?"

Benedict cursed. "I don't know what came over me, and she's just so blasted irritating. She struck me, and then provoked me."

"Well then." Baldwyn folded his arms across his chest. "By all means make her cry, it seems you earned a bit of revenge."

Benedict groaned aloud. "What the devil are you doing here, Baldwyn? Don't tell me—"

"Agatha." They said in unison. Both as if her name was an expletive on their lips.

"She got to you, too, I imagine?" Benedict asked, though it was difficult to stay on topic after the feel of Katherine's lips on his own. He hadn't meant to hurt the girl's feelings, but she was so blasted…provoking. He'd said it aloud and continued to think it in his head.

Baldwyn snapped his fingers. "Woolgathering or planning to attack another virgin?"

"My apologies. You were saying?" Benedict shook his head and began walking in the direction of the whiskey with Paisley in tow.

Baldwyn had been raised alongside Benedict when they were children. Agatha was Baldwyn's grandmother and Benedict's aunt, making them cousins and, unfortunately, related to the same horrid woman that continued to meddle in the lives of the men in her family.

Benedict could think of only one reason why she would summon Baldwyn all this way.

"She's going to ruin the both of us." Benedict reached the whiskey and cursed. "Don't tell me she's turned her matchmaking sights to you cousin..." He waited, in vain, for Baldwyn to deny the accusations all together.

"I shall marry Lady Anastasia."

Benedict burst out laughing, sloshing his drink within the glass and nearly spilling it onto the Persian rug. "Truthfully? You are to marry her? Tell me, do you still have mud stains on your person? One would think they were permanent. Delightful creature that one. I have half a mind to cage her up with Katherine, at least they could torture one another instead of—" As the words came flowing out of his mouth Benedict realized in one horror-stricken moment, just what his aunt had done.

"She's betrothed us to..."

Baldwyn swallowed all of his brandy in one gulp. "Our enemies? Childhood nemesis? The only woman in London I could never imagine myself sharing a bed with? Yes, perhaps Agatha delights in having no heirs to speak of, for if I have to share a bed with that, that hoyden then I'm quitting."

Benedict scowled. "One cannot simply quit marriage."

"Did I say marriage? I meant quitting the continent."

"And your tenants will simply do without you for the remainder of their lives?"

Baldwyn poured another brandy. At this rate he was going to be foxed before he even had a dance, which surely would not do. "Must you be so logical when I'm this upset? At least try to see my plight. The girl probably still has pigtails. Do you remember the way her bony little hands used to pull at my coattails? She wasn't a bonny lass, and you know it. I think I may be sick."

"Yes, well..." Benedict took the empty glass from his cousin's hand. "Whiskey on an empty stomach will do that to you, now why don't you run along and find something to soak up all that alcohol while I have a nice friendly little chat with Agatha about your situation. There isn't much to be done about mine considering we were found..."

"Compromised?"

Benedict growled low in his throat. "As I said before, to everyone who would listen that is, I was unconscious, on the cold hard ground with nothing save a lump on the back of my head for my troubles! I did not seduce her!"

"Perhaps you've just gotten better at it."

Benedict lifted a brow.

"Just a thought, perhaps your sexual prowess is that of such brilliance that you are able to seduce women in your sleep."

"What a cross to bear," Benedict said dryly not finding his cousin amusing in the least.

"Yes well, I was trying to look at the positive in a very dreary situation. After all, the woman you have to marry nearly killed you thrice!"

"Ah, yes. Thank you for the reminder. I shall be sure to shout 'til death do us part quite proudly, knowing it will be quite soon in seeking me out."

"Speaking of the devil," Baldwyn mumbled and sauntered off in the other direction leaving Benedict alone in the room. He looked up and cursed fluently before downing the rest of his drink.

"Agatha."

"Benedict, I have just spoken with Katherine's parents

and they have denied your suit."

Odd, how such information could make one feel elated, yet offended all at once. "Whatever do you mean?"

Agatha lifted an eyebrow and took a seat on the nearest chair. "They find the idea of you marrying their only daughter quite offensive. In fact, they've instructed me to find her a suitable replacement considering you've already ruined her."

Appalled, Benedict could only stare slack-jawed. "But that's ridiculous! I ruined her, and I should be the one to pay for it! Granted, I wasn't necessarily awake for the entire act, but I'm pretty sure when a woman has her skirts up past her knees it's considered improper! What kind of parents are they? To subject their only daughter to such ridicule. And all because they find me offensive? Me? I'm a blasted duke!" Throwing an obvious tempter tantrum, he continued, "What the blazes is so awful about marrying me?" Other than the obvious.

His reputation for ruining debutantes.

His favor for strong drink and gambling.

And the rumor that he often walked around his manor naked in order to offend his valet, which might or might not have been true.

"That, my dear boy, was my exact question." Agatha inspected her gloves and shrugged as if she didn't know all the reasons a family would be less than thrilled to align themselves with him.

Did that mean the witch was actually siding with her nephew? Impossible!

"And?" Benedict prompted.

"It isn't so much the parents whom object as it is the girl in question. She claims you are the most boring creature to walk the face of the earth. She also finds your inability to smile quite taxing."

Benedict's blood boiled. "For the last time, I know how to smile!"

"Don't shout, my dear, I'm sitting right here." Agatha shuddered. "Either way, I've taken care of it for you."

Devil's teeth. Those were words one never wanted to hear from one's insane aunt. The same aunt that thought it stylish to fasten feathers to her lap dog.

Agatha smiled. "I've merely suggested you pay court to their daughter until the Kringle Ball in two weeks' time. If, by then, you've failed in all aspects of intelligent conversation and of course, managed not one smile, which I do think will be a challenge, then the betrothal is off."

Benedict opened his mouth to curse, as well as tell his aunt exactly what he thought about her little deal, but her loud voice cut him off.

"She was found, on top of you, Benedict, at a society function. Have a care for her reputation and at least see this through. Imagine what your mother would say."

With that, Agatha rose to her feet and exited the room. The slamming of the door sounding much like the final nail in his bachelor's coffin. For, Agatha, manipulative little thing that she was, knew his weakness. The one weakness he had.

His deceased mother.

He cursed again and followed Agatha out of the room.

Chapter Five

Foxed

Katherine wanted to cry, but to waste tears on such a horrid man seemed truly ridiculous. Dabbing at her eyes, considering they were going to turn into watering pots in any minute, she took a deep breath and walked back into the ballroom.

Her father and mother had just spent the past half hour trying to convince her of the smart match with the Banbury. She had argued until he throat was sore, giving every excuse under the sun, violence not included for obvious reasons, that they were ill-suited for one another.

When, in desperation she finally did mention the accidents that befell the duke every time in her presence, her mother merely asked, "Could you at least try to be less clumsy? Perhaps if you practiced."

"I do not think I understand your meaning," Katherine had said, her voice filled with dread.

"What your mother is trying to say…" Her father cleared

his throat and looked off into the distance. "Perhaps if you tried to be more feminine. You know, learned how to properly walk instead of stomping all over the place. Decided not to speak your mind. You know what I'm saying." He cleared his throat again. "Dumb yourself down so that other fellows don't feel so intimidated, then you would make a good match. The Devil Duke would have to marry you then. He'd have nothing to object to."

"It is I who object to him!" Katherine said through clenched teeth.

"Of course, my dear." Her mother patted her hand. "So what shall we tell him?"

In the end, they had come up with a compromise, if he could win their daughter before the Kringle's ball, they would marry. If not, well, if not then Katherine would still be in a pickle, because by all accounts she was still ruined.

Unless, the Duke of Banbury denied all accusations. But even if he did, people would still stare and wonder what did go on that night.

Her parents left her to make herself presentable, which was quite difficult considering she had a blasted headache and her ankle hurt. In the end, she only managed to pinch her cheeks and walk out into the ballroom.

And now she was trying not to cry for the third time that night. What she wouldn't give to punch the man in the face. He didn't want her, and it seemed nobody would now that she had been ruined by the very man mamas warned their daughters about.

Who would want a girl that even the Devil chose not to marry?

She took a shaky breath. Lovely first meeting. Tonight she had every intention of gaining the attention of the Scottish duke. Now, she was limping, betrothed, and ready to yell at any man who dare cross her path.

"Hullo there! You must be Lady Katherine!" an irritating voice bellowed behind her. Slowly, she turned. A man, a very attractive man, stood not five feet away from her. Cheeky grin in place, he gave a quick bow. "May I steal you for a dance?"

She wanted to say no, she really did, it was on the tip of her tongue, not that the man was disagreeable; he was actually quite handsome, if one liked dark red hair and blue eyes. But, the last thing she wanted was to have a meaningless conversation when she was still trying to keep her eyes from tearing up.

And then, she saw him. Across the room. Lips in a firm line of hatred. Lovely, perhaps he would smite her with his smolder. One could only hope, at least in heaven she wouldn't be betrothed.

"I'd love to," she heard herself say, then glared back at Benedict. His scowl said it all. He actually kicked the floor before disappearing behind another couple.

Unbelievable.

Katherine returned her gaze to the man she'd just agreed to dance with. His beauty was actually quite flawless, if one liked dandies or perhaps fops. His waistcoat glowed, causing her eyes to burn just slightly. But that was the result when one was wearing a bright yellow piece of clothing. Perhaps he was color blind? He led her to the middle of the ballroom floor and bowed. She stifled a snort when the couple next to them scowled. Truthfully, it wasn't necessary to bow that low unless she was royalty.

He was still facing the floor as the music started, and then with a sweeping gesture he pulled her into his arms.

Winded, for they were moving vigorously in the wrong direction of the steps, Katherine managed a tight smile and grunted when they stepped toward one another and he stepped on her toes.

Goodness, did she have to endure an entire dance with

this man?

Apparently, she did. Perhaps this was her punishment for succumbing to the Devil Duke's charms. Truthfully, she had no idea what had come over her, and then to have Baldwyn see it all, well it was turning out to be the worst night of her life, and then...

"May I cut in?" the Duke of Paisley's deep timbre sent a shudder down her spine. She paused in the dance and looked up. He was making an absolute scene. Mayhap he did have feelings for her? But hadn't his engagement just been announced?

So, she was to be the pity dance.

Lovely.

Always great to know when she was wanted by the man she loved the most.

Her dandified partner, whose name she still hadn't been given, glared, and hopped off. Literally had a hop in his step as he tried to storm the room.

The music continued to drift, dancers swirled around her and the Scottish duke held out his gloved hand.

So this was what it felt like to want and not have.

Reluctantly, she put her hand in his as he gently pulled her into the dance with a smoothness unmatched by any man except his cousin, the very man she did not wish to think of. Paisley had always been the kind one when they were little, and now he was looking upon her the same way Banbury did—pity and not an inch of attraction. Had she really changed so little? The thought darkened her mood, perhaps that was why she was labeled a spinster. She had offers, but none of them were from her heart's true desire. Suddenly depressed, she grimaced.

"Are you alright?" he asked smoothly. His face was turned away from hers as if watching. With his red cheeks and blazing eyes, she wasn't sure if he was foxed or just plain irritated.

"I'm fine, t-thank you," she stuttered as she took another sweeping step.

"Don't know why it's my lot in life to have to save every simpering female within the realm. Have you any idea who that man was?"

"A dandy?" she guessed.

He did not look amused, instead his eyes took on more fury, drilling a hole through her very person. "That was Sir Elliot himself, the very same man, who just a few weeks ago, was found ravaging the very young Lady Lillian Derby."

"Him?" Katherine tried not to look amused, but the idea of that man ravishing anything was inconceivable. "And here I thought it was Banbury who did all the ruining."

"Looks can be quite deceiving, and believe me, Banbury isn't without his faults, but when it comes to women, he has more of a mature taste." His eyes scanned her from head to toe as if to say, "Pity, you aren't one of them." He shrugged and continued to glare in the opposite direction toward the wall.

"How is the girl?" Katherine asked needing to change the subject before she burst into tears. Is that how all men saw her? First she was a spinster, and now she was hardly a woman! Not even good enough for the Devil Duke to freely ruin and not good enough for Paisley either.

"Ruined, at the young age of one and six. You would do well to stay away from him."

At least he would try to ruin her, whereas everyone else found her disagreeable.

"Noted." She gulped and took one last turn just as Benedict's voice rose above the music.

Paisley's eyes searched the crowd until they landed on Benedict. Cheeks ruddy and stance not at all sturdy, the man was completely and utterly foxed.

What a grand night this had turned out to be.

Katherine pulled away, thoroughly disgusted with not only her behavior but that of her betrothed, and to be honest, a little heartsick that the very man she had loved since she was a small girl was doing nothing but a small favor. Protecting her as if she was still a girl of nine years.

Had nobody noticed that she was a woman? Did she need to shout it just as Benedict was shouting now?

Though he wasn't using words, merely grunts, and thankfully the music was loud enough to drown out some of his bellow.

He reached her side and pulled her aggressively across his body, sending a seething glare to Paisley before using her as a crutch to leave the room.

She said nothing.

Katherine kept silent, which was a small miracle in and of itself, and helped Benedict to the doors leading outside. It was when she reached the double doors that she stole a glance back at Paisley, whose eyes were trained on Lady Anastasia as if she was his water in a drought. Would any man ever look at her with such hunger? For she did not miss the way his eyes hooded the minute they set upon Lady Anastasia. She felt herself blush as she looked back down at the ground feeling suddenly very much an imposter.

Heartsick, she swallowed the lump in her throat and helped Banbury down the remaining stairs.

He slurred for his carriage.

Katherine rolled her eyes.

This was her life. Helping the drunken Devil Duke into his carriage while licking her wounds from the other duke who was too pigheaded to do anything worthwhile and thought her nothing but a schoolgirl.

The fact that they were both foxed and angry just irritated her all the more.

The carriage seemed to take years. The footman jumped

down to help the duke into the carriage.

"Good riddance," she uttered under her breath as she turned on her heel.

"Wait," Banbury called, his voice strangely quiet.

Against her better judgment, she stopped in her tracks. With a resigned sigh, she turned back to the carriage and leaned in.

"I forgot…" Banbury ran a gloved hand through his perfectly dark hair.

"What did you forget?"

"My betrothed."

With strength of a god, he pulled her into the carriage, causing her to tumble across his lap, and the blasted horses took off.

If she wasn't ruined before, she was good and ruined now. Her last thoughts before the Devil Duke brought her to his lap and kissed her.

Chapter Six

To Dare the Duke

One kiss, just one blasted kiss.

Blind rage had engulfed his entire body when he saw Baldwyn dancing with Katherine. An emotion he had never before experienced slammed into his chest, stealing the breath straight from him. Unable to speak, he had resorted to bellowing in the large ballroom rather than politely walking up to the couple and punching his cousin in the face.

Truthfully, everyone within the vicinity was lucky he was foxed, for even he was not drunk enough to falsely believe he would be a good shot. Not with how heavy his body had felt.

It was all Rawlings' fault, for he had found great amusement in goading Benedict to drink more. And then Renwick had joined in, and some other gentleman who had a twin, and to be honest, it was all quite fuzzy after that.

Montmouth told him he should sleep it off.

And he was going to.

Really he was.

Until he saw her.

Heaven above, she was beautiful, and she really didn't have a right to be anything but disagreeable and ugly. After all, she had nearly killed him and then ruined him, a renowned scoundrel of all people, in front of his aunt!

Without logic entering into the equation, he grabbed the minx by the arm and brought her outside.

His only goal to scare her and warn her of dalliances with other men. If he was to placate her family, he needed to have his two weeks without any competition. Not that he was worried he would lose, it just didn't seem fair.

But once he opened his mouth, her vanilla scent bombarded him nearly sending him to his knees, and once again he was filled with a violent lust that left him wondering what it would feel like to lick her bare skin.

Unfortunately, he was too foxed to use any of his usual tactics.

Meaning, he resorted to trickery.

Not one of his finer moments.

She didn't even fight him.

Which, according to his drunken haze, told him she desired him as much as he desired her, which according to his calculations, also meant she would be receptive to his kiss.

She wasn't.

Instead, she pushed against his chest and kicked until, with a curse, he pulled away.

"What the devil was that for?"

"You pompous, arrogant, son of a—"

His hand covered her mouth before she made a fool of herself by insulting a peer of the realm, one that ranked higher than her, if only by a tiny hair.

"Cease from speaking, you insulting wench." Well, he could have said that better. He blamed the whiskey, and those two wretched twins. What were their names again? Anthony and Ambrose, something? Why the devil did they keep pouring that whiskey? Terrible idea to begin with. He needed a clear mind, not one muddled with alcohol.

He shook his head.

Katherine slapped him, offering her assistance no doubt.

"Well, that was helpful, my thanks." He scowled and touched his cheek where he carried a painful mark of her assault.

"What the devil do you think you're doing?" Katherine's nostrils flared. He didn't need to be sober to know she was upset, but he did need to be sober to be able to concentrate on her face rather than the swell of her breasts.

Blast, but she had nice breasts.

All round and...

"Benedict!" she screamed his Christian name quite loudly. What the devil did she do that for? Had she no care for the foxed?

"Stop yelling!" he yelled.

"Why did you kidnap me like that? I'm completely and utterly ruined now! My parents are probably already announcing our engagement, elated that I left with you! Oh, this is so horrible!" She sat back against the cushions and punched the seat with her hand.

"Yes well, I obviously hadn't thought that through very well," he admitted touching a hand yet again to his throbbing face.

"You don't say?" she mocked.

"Now see here." His head felt much clearer when he was enraged, funny that. "We will marry and that is that."

"Hours ago, you wanted to murder me, and now you want to marry me?"

"Yes, well no, I'm not sure."

"I feel so desired, la, I'm going to be a puddle at your feet if you keep speaking to me with such delicate words and phrases."

"You don't want to marry me," he stated boldly. "You've told your parents and my aunt, though you grudgingly admitted to allowing me two weeks to court you."

"I thought it a kindness." She smiled sweetly.

Minx. "No, you thought to inflict more torture on my person. But not again, I will not be ruined and then jilted out of a proposal."

"Pardon?" She leaned forward.

"You heard me, I was quite ruined tonight."

"What?"

"Ah, so she lacks intelligence as well as hearing?" Benedict grinned at his brilliance. "You ruined me, not the other way around. It was you on top of me, and you who clumsily fell into my carriage; all it would take is one word from me to your family and you'd be stuck with me."

Katherine folded her arms across her chest, giving him another lovely view he wouldn't mind staring at for the remainder of the evening. "Smarter when you're foxed, hmm?"

His eyes darted back up to her face. He really needed to stop getting so distracted. "I'm always smarter, and don't you forget it. The way I see things is you have no choice but to marry me. But never fear. I will allow you to earn the right to choose and court me as you see fit."

"Me?" Katherine laughed. "Court you? A man? How much whiskey did you consume?"

Not near enough, not near enough. Blazes, her smile was beautiful. Why was it so blasted hot in that carriage? He cleared his throat. "I'll call upon you tomorrow and you may court me as you see fit."

"Or else?" she asked in a tiny voice.

"Or else I'll ruin you even more than you're ruined at this very moment. You won't be accepted anywhere, and my slip of a cousin will be sorry he ever danced with you.

A defeated look washed across her features as her eyebrows drew together and her mouth gaped open. "I know what you're doing."

He sure hoped not.

"You, you!" She pointed at him and pounded the cushion again. Poor, sad, little cushion seat. "You mean to make it look like it's my fault when the engagement doesn't work! You mean to salvage your pride, you hateful man!"

He sneered. "But of course, it works for the both of us. Your parents see that you truly tried to make it work, you put forth such a gallant effort. And in the end, when it still isn't enough to win over the most infamous duke of the *ton*, they'll nurse your broken heart, and you will be free to do whatever you like."

"But—" She chewed her lower lip. What he wouldn't give to be that lip.

Water, he needed some sort of water to get rid of his foxed state. He was starting to feel…sentimental. "But, I'll still be ruined, won't I?"

"Of course." He grinned. What did he care if she was ruined? He already planned on ruining her, ravishing her, and then leaving. That was to be her punishment for all the torture she'd put him through, and she was more than deserving. He would enjoy every single second.

She took a deep breath and cursed, quite impressively for a young lady.

"You're the devil," she said.

"So I've been told, love. So I've been told." He picked up her hand though she tried to keep it at her side, and bestowed a kiss across her knuckles. "And always at your service, should you need to make another deal with the devil." With a wink, he pulled back, chuckling.

Chapter Seven

A Deal is Made

Katherine narrowed her eyes at the man. Surely he was the devil himself! The injustice of it all. By all appearances it would look—well, it would look like she was besotted with the man, and then when it would be time for them to announce their betrothal, there would be no betrothal to announce. Her parents would be livid, she would still be utterly ruined, and Benedict would get away scot free, Devil Duke reputation intact, and if anything, even more famous throughout the *ton*!

But worse of all, her heart dropped as her mind played the truth over and over again in her head. The Duke of Paisley would be out of reach, for even if he wasn't already betrothed to Lady Anastasia, what would he possibly want with a ruined girl?

So, it was in that moment, when she looked at the choices laid out before her, that she became selfish and impulsive. If no one was to have her, if love would never be her destiny, perhaps she could make the duke's life a living, waking nightmare. For it was his fault that this was all coming to pass.

"Why are you smiling?" he asked, grinning and leaning forward to receive a kiss, no doubt.

"Oh, because." She gave him her most coy look and blinked her eyes, resting them finally on his lips as her eyelashes fluttered. She looked back up, into his piercing gaze.

Eyes dilated, his gaze was ravenous, dark, sensual. She gulped and leaned forward. His lips met hers in a frenzy. She reciprocated, allowing herself one moment of weakness before biting his bottom lip, hoping she would draw blood.

The duke cursed. "What the devil was that for?"

"Ruining my happiness, that's what. Good day, your grace, it seems we have two weeks to become acquainted. Get your beauty rest, for you'll need it."

He cursed again as the carriage came to a halt in front of her house. "Oh, and Banbury?" She stepped out of the carriage and turned. "Consider yourself warned. I never back down without a fight."

"Been nearly killed thrice to prove that very true statement," he muttered begrudgingly.

"Exactly." She winked and walked into the house.

Not one to throw any sort of tantrums, Katherine stomped up the stairs and quietly closed her bedroom door, all the while forcing her mind to forget the feel of the devil's lips as they caressed her own.

Why was he nicknamed the Devil Duke anyway? Granted, he leaned toward rakish tendencies and did have a slight obsession with horse racing, but didn't all fashionable young gentleman?

The way things looked tonight, the men of London were drinking whiskey as if it was going out of style and slapping one another on the back as if being a man was such a brilliant privilege that they needed to keep congratulating one another on their sex.

Katherine knew she needed to get her rest, for tomorrow would be the most trying day of all. For at dawn, she had to begin courting the devil himself and every able-minded person in London would sit back and watch the entertainments, for she would be the first woman to ever gain a proposal from the duke.

****

Knock, knock, knock. Benedict lifted his pounding head, rising slowly from the warmth of his bed. The knocks began anew.

He cursed.

"I know you're in there!" the voice boomed.

Agatha.

Well, now it was final. She was singlehandedly trying to kill him. Had she no respect for the inebriated and half dead? He blinked several times and rubbed his eyes just as the door burst open. Agatha entered with his irritated valet, Percy, in tow.

"How could you?" she screamed again affirming his earlier assumption that she was planning his demise.

"How could I, what?"

"Be such a man!"

He wasn't sure if he should be pleased or horrified that his aunt had accused him of such. He looked down to make sure at least half of his body was covered and sighed in relief that he was.

"Did you want me to be a woman?"

Percy coughed.

Agatha narrowed her gaze. "Your very presence irritates me."

Benedict sighed. "So it seems. I take it this is the reason for your intrusion? My offensive sex and irritating presence. Pray, if I offend you so, why don't you simply leave?"

She snorted and stomped her heel onto Percy's foot.

Eyes wide, Percy clenched his teeth and slowly lifted his eyes heavenward.

God does not hear our pleas my friend, believe me, I've tried, Benedict thought.

"You are not listening to me!" Agatha yelled.

Any louder and his head might explode. Then again, if he died he wouldn't have to listen to Agatha screech anymore.

"Apologies, you were saying something about irritation and my offending sex?"

"You've made a horrible mess of everything! Do you even know what people are saying? It's all over the gossip rags. Oh, heavens. You've done some terrible things, Benedict, but this truly takes the cake!" She thrust a paper in his face and lifted a handkerchief to her eyes.

Benedict took the paper and scowled.

It was Mrs. Peabody's blasted gossip rag. Everyone read it. He would be lying if he said this was his first offense, the chit clearly had it out for him. With an exaggerated sigh, he read the words:

This should come as no shock to the rest of you. This author, however, was utterly appalled. To think! The Devil Duke ruining an innocent, and at the holiday's first ball! Shamefully, I was beginning to think rumors of this dark duke's demeanor were merely exaggerated. Now I believe we can all see firsthand what type of man he is.

For a man who not only ruins a woman in front of his own flesh and blood, but has the audacity to capture her and enclose her within the confines of his carriage sans chaperone, *can only be one thing. A devil in disguise. This author only hopes that the matriarch of that particular family will do something before the devil does more*

damage. La, I have it on good authority that it would take the fires of hell licking at his heels before the duke would say yes to an engagement. In case you were keeping track, dear readers, this brings a grand total of ten ruined debutantes over the course of three years. This author shudders to think of the disgrace heaped on both families. Well, it is positively not done! If he is given more invitations for the holidays, this author may eat her quill!
~Mrs. Peabody's Society Papers

Benedict laughed, amused that the lady would accuse him so hotly of something that was truly not even his fault.

She accosted him.

She fell on him.

She leaned in and kissed him.

Fine, so the last part was slightly exaggerated, but still, she was just as guilty. No woman should have such soft lips.

"What will you do?" Agatha asked, arms crossed.

By the look in her eyes he knew he had one of two choices. Laugh it off and kick her out of his home with a hearty farewell or make her privy to his true intentions. After all, he did have some pride to salvage. To think, a woman denying him…and a spinster no less!

"I'm so pleased you've asked, and to think I was just readying myself to come over to your house and tell you of my plans."

Agatha rolled her eyes. "Which is why you were still sleeping when I knocked on the door."

"I was merely meditating on the sweet words I would utter to my beloved."

It was Percy's turn to snort, and Agatha coughed behind her hand.

"Besides," Benedict added with a stretch, "To say what happened against my door was a knock would be a terrible injustice. It was more of a bang, or something akin to a cannon exploding in my bedchamber. Now if you will be so kind as to excuse me, I have a call to make."

With determination, he offered a smile.

He wasn't sure if it was the smile or the speech, but his aunt promptly fainted.

Three hours later, after an ungodly amount of smelling salts, tea, and instances when he saw his aunt's ankles, she was packed into a carriage and sent home.

"Do you think she was feigning illness?" Baldwyn said beside him. Apparently Benedict hadn't been the only one to be roused from his sleep in the early morning. In fact, Baldwyn had smartly chosen to break his fast at Benedict's home while Agatha stormed into Benedict's rooms to scold him.

Baldwyn had it easy, however. He simply needed to speak to the girl's father and all would be done.

Benedict had to fight.

But he was used to winning.

And how difficult could it be to win a spinster's heart?

Chapter Eight

Try Again

Katherine pleaded with her parents to allow her to return to the country. Instead, it seemed the more she begged, the more resolute they were in their decision.

Upset, she had taken to her rooms.

A knock sounded at her door.

Please let it be a thief coming to steal her away or perhaps knock her senseless? And then she could wake up confused as to how she was ruined the night before.

She wanted to forget any of it happened.

It was too mortifying.

Too horrible.

Everything, except the stolen kisses.

But they didn't count. Everyone knew kisses only counted when they were given in earnest, and if Benedict was earnestly kissing her, well, the whole idea would be ludicrous.

He was merely competitive and a seducer of innocents

and truly the worst sort of man. Well, he had been successful in ruining her and now the only course of action was to go about a betrothal and wait for him to inevitably end things. Then she could go back to the country and die alone.

Splendid.

Not exactly how she imagined her life would turn out.

"Enter," she said, thoroughly disgusted with herself for entertaining dreams of the rogue's kisses.

"He's here."

Katherine picked a feather off of her pillow and huffed. "Who?"

"You told me not to utter his name," her maid, Nancy, said in a tiny voice.

Shivering, Katherine sat up. "You mean *he's* here?"

"The very one."

"Well, who let him in?" she all but screamed.

"Your mother. Seems she was overwrought after the scandal sheets were delivered. Allow me to speak frank."

"Always."

"It is worse than you thought upon returning last night, my lady."

"How much worse?" Katherine asked, sick with dread.

"Much."

Well, that was descriptive and helpful. She had to think. Her eyes darted to the window.

"I fear the fall would kill you." Nancy read her thoughts.

Drat.

Allowing herself a few minutes of silent pity, Katherine closed her eyes and sighed. Things could always be worse. She could be deathly ill, or perhaps crippled, or blind or…

She shuddered. After all, it was never a good sign when one had to think of death in comparison to her current situation.

Katherine managed to make it down the stairs, though

she took great pains to methodically count each step, for in her mind, it was a reminder of how many steps she would take until she entered the inferno.

How was it, she wondered, that God allowed such a man to live?

Upon entering the room, she was given her answer.

For like Lucifer himself, the man was too beautiful to kill.

Curse him.

"Ah, my dear, there you are!" Her father embraced her and patted her on the head. But Katherine's eyes never left the duke's.

"Your grace." She curtsied quickly and walked behind the sofa to put distance between them. Merciful heavens, why weren't there any windows open?

"If I may be so bold, you look extravagant this morning, my lady." Benedict gave her a stare that made her heart flutter in all the wrong places. Treacherous body! Perhaps she should have taken her luck with the fall out of the window.

"You may not be so bold," Katherine clipped. "Especially when you freely give such compliments without as much as smiling."

"Apologies." He grimaced, though to be fair it was probably the closest to a smile she was going to get.

"Yes, well, as long as it doesn't happen again."

"Katherine!" Her mother scolded. "After everything that has transpired, do you not think you should show a little more favor to the duke? After all, as of an hour ago you are officially engaged."

Suddenly glad she was leaning on the settee, Katherine sputtered, "S-surely not!"

Benedict's eyes shimmered with merriment as he narrowed his gaze and approached her. "But, my dear, you seemed so much more keen on the idea last night."

Fists planted firmly at her sides, it took every ounce of

strength not to lash out at the man. He wanted this marriage less than she did. What the devil was he up to? What happened to the two weeks' time in which she had to court him, and he was going to cry off like the fool he was?

"Then perhaps you should refresh my memory, for I do not remember hearing any sort of proposal from your lips."

"No," he leaned in to whisper in her ear. Why weren't her parents doing anything? She looked from left to right. Drat, they had abandoned her, and the door was closed. Well, there was no way out of this one. She would just have to fight.

She pushed against him; he grasped her clenched hands. "So you want me to refresh your memory, do you?" His breath tickled her ear.

"If you touch me, I'll scream."

"Not the first time a woman's felt the need to do that in my presence, I assure you. Besides, with my certain skill set, your mother will simply blush profusely all the while fanning herself, and your father would be more likely to pat me on the back than shoot me."

"How can you be so sure of yourself?"

"Because." A smug look crossed his chiseled face. "I promised to fix everything."

Interesting that he would do anything so noble. "Just what do you intend to fix?"

"First, I'm going to fix this business about ruining you. Second, I'm going to pretend to be infatuated, though it won't be terribly hard considering you kiss like a courtesan. And third? Third, I'm going to get to the bottom of this business with my aunt trying to pair us up."

Katherine burst out laughing. Oh, the poor deluded man. "Your aunt was doing nothing of the sort, you arrogant beast!"

"Clearly, you've hit your head." Benedict stepped back and folded his arms across his chest. "She told me I was to be married, and mentioned you'd…"

Suddenly his face went very white.

"Mentioned what? Our names in the same sentence? Believe me, your aunt would never align us. She had much higher aspirations for me."

Benedict grabbed her shoulders turning her ever so slightly closer to his body. "Explain."

"She penned a note about the Winter's Festivities and mentioned to my parents how eager she was for me to meet the Duke of Paisley."

"Paisley? But he's to be with…"

While he was making calculations, she stepped back out of his reach. The man was too handsome by half, and it seemed near impossible to think in his presence. It was why she was always so clumsy around him. Paisley had always been kind to her as a child, and Benedict, well, he brooded and girls swooned.

At least now when he brooded, they guarded their virtue with fans.

"Look at it this way, your grace. It seems your aunt deemed Paisley good enough to have a choice between me and Lady Anastasia. I'm sorry all I have is the information given me, but I do not believe she was trying to trap you, at least not with me."

"Why not with you?" he roared.

Why the devil was he allowed to be offended?

Why not, indeed. "Because I'm a Kerrington, and we do not associate with rakes."

"You're a spinster."

"I'm a woman."

"I think we've established that thrice."

"The same amount of times I've accosted you. Interesting." Katherine moved to the door, but his hand slammed across the knob.

"Am I that blackened? Tell me you didn't dream of my

kiss, don't want my hands on your body. Tell me you don't desire me, and I'll restore your reputation and cry off, forgetting this whole business."

Her body screamed for her to give in to his touch, his masculine scent of soap and tobacco, the gleam in his eyes that promised wicked pleasure.

But as soon as she allowed herself the image of what it would be like to be in his arms, her mind conjured up Paisley. If there was a chance, however slight, that she could be with him...

She cleared her throat. "The only thing I feel for you is revulsion, and that is the truth."

He blinked at her before stepping back, and looked again at her face as if confused. He opened the door and took a deep breath, giving her one final glance. It didn't seem possible, but his eyes held pain.

Perhaps the man had feelings after all.

Chapter Nine

Impossible Suddenly Quite Possible

Benedict walked to his carriage in silence.

He couldn't find the words to say anything, not even "Whites," which was exactly where he wanted to go, but truthfully if his footman suddenly had an inkling to go to the moon, Benedict would have been more than willing.

Anything to get rid of this ridiculous itch on his chest.

Well, perhaps it wasn't on his chest.

More like inside his chest, not truthfully an itch, more like a feeling, cursed word that it was.

And if he was being honest with himself, it felt quite a lot like the day his nanny chose to give Paisley a new toy and scolded Benedict for being naughty.

Then again, this feeling was much worse. It was hard to breathe, as if each time he opened his mouth he was only able to suck in so much air before his lungs collapsed altogether.

His footman waited patiently.

"Whites," he finally croaked, thankful he was able to at

least get that much out.

When had that chit gained the upper hand?

His mind was fuzzy as to how a person could outsmart him, and a woman no less. Had she any idea who he was? What he could do to her if he so chose?

Perhaps he felt positively ill because he knew exactly what Agatha was up to. Never would he consider her mad again, for she had played her cards well.

She had set up a trap, and he had fallen quite perfectly for the bait. Whatever she was up to, he would find out.

The rub, it seemed, was that he truthfully could do nothing to salvage Katherine's reputation. It was good and ruined, which really was a pity. Reputations should be ruined for good reason, not stolen kisses or happy accidents, or in his case, assault.

No, it seemed only fair that she be well and truly ruined, the way a woman with lush curves and pouty lips should be.

In bed.

He laughed.

Most likely his footman now thought him mad, but he didn't care.

His conscience nagged at him, stupid thing that it was. He had tried to dispel it years ago to no avail.

How was he to ruin a girl already ruined, who despised him and to whom he was also engaged?

Well, he was always one for puzzles.

Now all he needed was some very strong tea and a few hours to come up with a plan. Yes, she would rue the day she told the Devil Duke she had no feelings for him. She would rue the day she told him "no".

****

That night, as Katherine sat opposite her parents in the

carriage, she could not shake the feeling of dread in her belly.

Benedict would be attending this night's opera.

She was still ruined.

The *ton* would be waiting for a scandal, and worst of all, Paisley would be given a front row seat.

"Here we are." Her mother beamed when their carriage pulled up to King's Theatre.

Katherine bit her lip trying to keep the fluttering of her stomach at bay, and slowly made her way into the opera house.

It was too loud for her to be noticed, with too many people fluttering about.

"…and he has been ever so gracious to let us use his box!" Her mother clapped her hands together.

"Who?" Katherine loudly asked, for she could barely hear herself think.

"Why, the duke, of course."

"Which one?"

Her mother paused. "Have you so quickly forgotten the name of your *fiancé*?"

Oh, *him*. "No, apologies. It seems I've become quite… flushed."

Her mother scowled. "I knew I should not have left you alone this morning with that dreadful man. His reputation is black as sin, but surely you know there is no other choice?"

Katherine nodded.

"Did he…make advances toward you?"

Eyes wide, she could only shake her head *no* and pray her blush wasn't as bright as it felt. It would do no good for her mother to know the specifics. Besides, it wasn't as if she wanted her mother to die of an apoplexy.

No, she'd leave the dying to Benedict.

But then again…

Why wouldn't her heart stop fluttering?

"This way." Her father directed them to the box. At least there were only six seats. Enough for her parents, herself, Banbury and…

"The Dowager Duchess of Durbin," the lady introduced herself to her mother and father, then quickly darted her beady eyes in Katherine's direction.

"My dear, you look ever so lovely."

Katherine blushed again, and reached out to grasp the dowager's hands, leaning in to kiss both of her rouged cheeks.

"Your grace, it has been an age. I've missed you dreadfully."

A cough was heard near the front of the balcony.

All heads turned in the direction of the interruption.

"Apologies, seems I've come down with the ague." Benedict shrugged and winked at his aunt, whose icy glare caused the group to take a step back.

Benedict didn't seem the least bit affected. "We are so pleased to have you with us this evening." His voice dripped with sarcasm. The man was a conundrum, from his black attire, to the way his eyes scanned each person before him as if studying them.

Katherine cleared her throat to take a seat, on the opposite side of the box, but a hand stopped her.

"Katherine," her mother whispered harshly in her ear. "It will look dreadful if you do not sit next to your *fiancé*. Do not make this worse than it already is."

It could get worse. It could get *much* worse. For one thing, Benedict could have her skirts lifted merely by crooking his pinky finger.

She was a wanton hussy.

The man had no shame, and no right to be as attractive as he was. Why was it that men who had impossible personalities were gifted with good looks? Should it not be the other way around?

Then again, Paisley was quite handsome and kind and...
You're not marrying Paisley, you nitwit!

"Your grace." Katherine curtsied before taking a seat next to Benedict. The lights soon dimmed, and she found herself in quite an interesting position.

For the close proximity seemed to cause a sensual current between the two of them. His thigh barely brushed hers, but he didn't seem the least bit affected. He crossed his arms and leaned back as if bored. While she, well, she was near trembling.

And then the odious man stretched, just grazing her shoulder as his arm flew above his head. When his hands came down, a finger brushed hers.

This was why they called him the devil. This very reason, for he was able to conjure up nonsensical feelings with a mere touch.

"Tell me." She jumped as his lips barely touched her ear. "What is it you're thinking of? We both know you haven't even glanced at the performance."

"If you must know," she hissed, "I was just wondering where Paisley was located. Your aunt expressed her desire for us to continue our acquaintance."

"Paisley?" he all but spat. "He's engaged, as are you."

"According to you, all I had to do was deny my attraction, and you would cry off."

He shrugged. "I lied. Besides, you're already ruined. The way I see it, I'm doing you a favor merely by sitting with you."

She hated that he was right.

"Does he make you feel...things?"

"Who?"

"Paisley."

"Of course. I feel quite happy when I am near him, which is more than I can say about you."

Benedict chuckled, his finger drawing a slow circle on her

arm. "I do not want you to feel happy when you are near me."

"What a dreadful thing to say—"

"I merely want you to feel…" He paused. "Alive."

Any more alive and she would be quite dead from want.

"You cannot force a person to desire you, as you well know," she said haughtily, her voice jumping a few octaves to prove her offense. She refused to look at him and kept her eyes on the performance.

"My dear, who said anything about forcing?" His teeth nipped her ear just as she gasped and the crowd broke out in applause.

The first act was done.

She wasn't so sure she would make it through the rest.

****

Benedict couldn't see straight, and it had nothing to do with whiskey, but everything to do with the minx sitting next to him.

Had a courtesan dressed her?

By Jove, she looked like…like…His mind was having trouble processing large words, and he struggled to remember to breathe at the same time, and considering he wanted to go on living, thank you very much, he chose not to think of an appropriate word.

"Beautiful," he muttered aloud without thought.

Her head snapped in his direction, which then made his snap back to the stage where the second act would be starting soon.

Well, now he looked like an overeager lad. Splendid.

A commotion was heard to his left a few boxes down.

Paisley.

Katherine flinched at his side. Was he imagining things or was the girl actually trying to slouch further into her seat?

Ridiculous.

"Hiding?" He jerked her upright with one fluid movement.

She glared. "Perhaps."

"It would never work, you know."

"What wouldn't?" The flicker of emotion in her eyes told him she knew exactly what he meant.

"You and Paisley. Unlike myself, he's a man of honor. Aunt has already announced his betrothal. You'd have to kill the girl in order to gain his hand in marriage, and even then I'd wager against you."

"Do you always offer such pretty compliments?" Her lower lip trembled. Blast, was the chit going to cry now?

"I'm merely telling you the truth. He is the honorable one."

"What does that make you?" Surprisingly her lip stopped trembling, her glassy eyes pierced him with such longing, he nearly forgot to breathe.

He swallowed, gaining time to gather himself. "It makes me the defiant one, I suppose."

She continued looking straight through him, making it deuced uncomfortable to do anything but stare back.

"Besides," he leaned in and prayed Agatha wasn't watching. "Do you truly believe he could bring you pleasure after you've experienced it with me?"

The minx smiled tightly. "Do you believe yourself to be the expert in that certain area, your grace?"

"I don't believe. I *know*."

She snorted.

Did she doubt him?

Of all the hair-brained notions. Had she any idea what type of man she was frivolously playing with?

****

"Come on." He jerked her to her feet and made apologies to the rest of their company. "The lady wants to take the air... absolutely stuffy here."

Heads nodded emphatically, and then she was out into the hall with the duke, absolutely pinned by his predatory stare.

He stretched out his arm, giving her no choice in the matter but to take it and hope they would return soon.

Dread filled her with each step away from the box that she took. Swallowing her fear, and to be honest, her excitement of being alone with the man, she continued on until he stopped in a darkened corner and pulled her in with him.

"Watch." He turned her toward the wall. Oh no, why hadn't she tried harder to fight him, or at least pulled away when he jerked her to her feet.

Trembling, she had only the option of hitting him in hopes to escape. Of course she had known him since he was a child, but obviously the man was different than the boy, and she always had a sort of fear of him.

"You've proved your point, now let me go." She moved to elbow him, but he slithered away.

"Point? What point?" He sounded quite confused.

"That you're not above terrifying innocent maidens into submission in order to gain what you want."

At that, he laughed, throwing his head back and then finally meeting her gaze, an actual smile of amusement on his face.

Katherine didn't mean to gasp, nor did she mean to lean forward to study the beautiful lines that made up this remarkable change in his demeanor, his deep set dimples, his wide smile.

Slowly, she lifted her hand and delicately touched his jaw.

Breath hissed between his teeth as he pushed her back against the wall she had just been just facing.

"Am I terrifying now?"

"Dreadfully."

He needn't know that she was more astonished at his smile than truly terrified.

"Good, though that wasn't why I went to all the trouble to bring you here. Now turn around like a good girl."

What in the blazes was he doing? Katherine slowly turned, aware of his every breath as Benedict's lips grazed her ear, his gloved hands moved to either side of her head, one lifted, and a small light entered into their alcove, enough to gain her bearings.

"We're so close to the stage."

"Yes, funny thing that, it seems this box hasn't been used for near a decade."

"Why?"

"Well." He pulled the curtains back even wider but not enough for them to be viewed by anyone. "It was said that Count Von Luxemburg killed his wife in this very box. Nobody has taken it since. It is also quite close to the middle class, which is of course, frowned upon."

Katherine nodded. "I see."

He tensed behind her.

"So you've taken me here to frighten me? To explain that if I don't marry you, my fate will be the same as the countess, is that right?"

"My, my." His hot breath scalded her neck. "What a fun little imagination you have packed up in here." His hand dipped into her coiffure, brushing her skull and causing tremors. "Unfortunately, I brought you to this abandoned box so you wouldn't need to stare at Paisley all night, and also so you could enjoy the opera."

"I *am* enjoying it," she fired back, clearly irritated.

"Really?" His whisper mocked her.

"Yes."

"Then what, pray tell, is the name of the opera?"

Katherine swallowed. Blast, she had no idea. Not one clue, but surely all operas were similar? "I don't remember, but it is very romantic."

His body shook with laughter behind her. "It's a comedy, minx. *Le Nozze de Figaro* to be exact, and I suspect that if you were truly paying attention, you would be quite entranced by the entire performance."

She grinned, and focused back at the stage. "What's happening?"

He didn't move during the entire act as his lips spoke delicately into her ear translating each movement, each song, as if it was his second nature. When she gasped and began laughing, he laughed with her, his body steel behind her.

The curtains closed, leaving them once again in utter darkness.

"We should return," Katherine whispered. "Surely, they will start to worry about us being alone for so long."

"Do you truly think it could get any worse?" he joked.

Katherine stifled a laugh. "Well, considering most the *ton* saw my skirts up past my knees…"

"Glorious looking knees, by the way. I would love to see them again," he interrupted.

"I thought you were unconscious."

"Perhaps I stole a peek."

"Rogue."

"Always."

Katherine shivered as his body left hers. She rubbed her arms at the sudden chill. What in the world was wrong with her?

The white of Benedict's gloves was visible in the darkened box. His hand slowly moved in front of him and then reached for the back of her head.

All was lost.

For she went willingly and quite wantonly into his arms. Not at all sure if it was he who had made the first move or she, and not caring even if she was the guilty party.

His lips parted, a hungry moan escaped them as he plundered her mouth with his tongue. A yearning shot through her at his erotic kiss, causing her hands to clench and tug at his hair. His mouth was hot and sweet, demanding in its pursuit.

Logic had nothing to do with the way she arched her back into his embrace, allowing easier access, and then when his hands began purposefully caressing down her chest, she was again lost. Sensations she never knew possible caused her knees to weaken.

Benedict nipped at her neck, and then cursed. "I cannot ruin you at an opera…"

She kissed him hard across the mouth.

"Devil take me…I so desperately want to try," he mumbled as he nibbled on her lower lip. "I doubt you would thank me come tomorrow morning, nor would you be ecstatic to face your parents once they see you completely disgraced."

She stiffened and retreated.

"Good choice," he uttered, mumbling another oath before taking an unsteady breath. "Blast, what the devil is wrong with me?"

Was he speaking rhetorically?

He cursed again, this time kicking something. "I cannot be walking around like some besotted fool, my aunt will have me by my b—" He coughed. "My neck, she'll have me by the neck, and I'll never hear the end of it."

"Your grace," Katherine spoke up.

But he was truly having a one-sided conversation, so he continued in justifying his actions. "It is your fault! If you were not a woman…"

Katherine snorted. "Would you rather I be a man?"

"No!" he sputtered. "No, no, no, no. Heavens no."

"I believe you." She covered her laugh.

Was he pacing? She could see movement but wasn't sure if he was pacing or merely throwing his fist in the air repeatedly.

"I know!"

She had an idea this was not going to end up being an intelligent end to their conversation.

"Hit me."

"Pardon?" she choked.

"Hit me, or trip me, anything really. I need to be reminded how utterly wrong you are for me, so that when I have moments of weakness, and don't deny it—I've had quite a few as of recently—I remember that we will not suit, we cannot suit."

"So your answer is violence?" she asked.

"Precisely. After all, you've threatened my life three times before, why not add a fourth?"

"Why not?" Katherine felt anger rise in her chest. The absolute cad! He would rather she strike him down than admit any sort of attraction?

Fine. He would get exactly what he asked for.

"It would be an honor, your grace." With that, she brought her fist back and landed a blow across his eye that would have done her father quite proud.

Chapter Ten

If Only Women were Allowed at Gentleman Jackson's...

To his utter shame and complete humiliation, Benedict took at least five minutes to regain consciousness. At least he suspected as much and wasn't willing to entertain the thought that it could have been longer. Being a man, it just wouldn't be kind.

The throbbing on his cheek and around the tender flesh of his eye screamed in protest as he gently touched the area where Katherine had hit him.

Clearly, she didn't need to be told twice to inflict pain. Though, to be fair, he had suspected she would merely give him a light pat across the shoulder or mayhap even kick him in the shin.

Not, to his great humiliation, give such a remarkable punch that he was rendered senseless for longer than he'd care to admit. Were they allowing women at Jackson's these days? He needed to stop underestimating the chit, his nemesis, his future wife. Bitter pill to swallow, that.

Breath whistled through his teeth as he set himself to rights and checked his body for any other sort of bruising. Naturally, he wouldn't put it past her to give a good kick after she sent him sailing to the ground.

Although sore, nothing else seemed worse for the wear, but he did have a sneaking suspicion he looked as if he had been on the wrong end of an opening door. With one final oath for good measure, he took another soothing breath and made his way back to the box.

Thankfully, everything was still blanketed in black. Unfortunately for him, he had the devil's own luck, so it wasn't all that surprising that the minute his booted foot stepped into his box, the stage lights came to life.

And he, the wounded, was no longer in darkness.

Rather blinded by the spectacle in front of him. His eyes focused on the stage and then to his horror, Agatha. Of course the witch was laughing.

"What the devil happened to you?" Agatha said between giggles. At least have a care for the company! What were they to think when she was not even a trifle concerned for his welfare!

"I took a stumble," he lied. His eyes quickly darted to Katherine.

The minx coughed. "And where pray tell did you stumble, your grace? Dare I ask the condition of the object that ran into your face?" She lifted her hand innocently to touch her cheek and winked. Not a blasted hair out of place. Gloves pristine.

He suddenly had a very vivid image of his hands shaking her tiny little body until she apologized.

Then again, he couldn't very well have her apologize for something he told her to do.

Stupidity seemed to blare in front of his eyes like a blazing sign.

"Benedict!" Agatha scolded. "Really! To leave Lady Katherine all by herself! Heavens! The poor dear was lost for near an hour while you were out fighting imaginary dragons!"

"I was attacked!" he shouted, bringing quite a lot of attention to their box. He swore and quickly took a seat so nobody would be the wiser to his bruise.

"Attacked?" Agatha's eyes narrowed. "Seconds ago you were most unfortunate to allow your clumsiness to get the best of you, and now you were accosted? By what, a child? A door?"

Katherine snorted behind her hand but kept her eyes dancing with amusement. Lord and Lady Kerrington were staring at him as if he had just sprouted an extra head near his ear.

"Well?" Agatha prodded.

"Both." He closed his eyes. "It was both. You see, I was trying to find Lady Katherine amidst the crowds—"

"—there were no crowds, Benedict, we were all seated."

"You did not let me finish!" He shifted in his seat. "The crowds of er...air." *Cough, cough.* "You see, the air was quite crowded with, dust, lots of dust, and you know I am allergic to dust, Aunt."

"Indeed."

At his silence she leaned in. "Oh, do go on, I believe your tale has just trumped my interest in the opera."

Lord Kerrington nodded his head in agreement. All eyes on him. He scratched nervously at his neck and cleared his throat. "As I said, the air was crowded with—"

"—dust, yes you've said that already," Katherine piped up cheerfully.

"Right." He clenched his teeth. "And by the time I was able to set myself to right and go in search of Katherine, who surely must have been confused because of all the..." He choked on his lie.

"Dust," they said in unison.

"Yes, dust," he said emphatically. "I wandered into a darkened corner, many of those in the theatre, you know, and promptly took a stumble. My eyes had not yet adjusted to the dust-free area."

Devil take him, he truly was the worst liar that ever lived. Plain and simple. Didn't help one bit that he was sweating through his jacket, nor that his aunt seemed to get more agitated by the minute.

Benedict leaned forward hoping to gain the attention of everyone and end this mortifying night. "I heard a scream."

"No!" Lady Kerrington gasped.

He smiled cheerfully. "Why yes, and I being the strong, courageous…"

"—Don't forget allergic," Katherine piped up again.

"Allergic," he ground out. "Ahem…man that I am, I went in search of the damsel. I'm happy to announce I made it just in time to save the woman in distress no worse for the wear!"

Odd nobody was clapping. Should he not be honored for his bravery, fake though it may be?

Agatha chuckled. "Interesting. For Katherine said both of you were merely lost and in a moment of panic she accidently hit you in the face because she thought she saw a rat."

"But," Benedict sputtered. "You asked…"

"Bravo!" Lord Kerrington slapped Benedict hard on the back. "Your Grace, my daughter was just regaling us with your ability to tell stories. I say, jolly good one! My dear," he looked to Katherine. "You were right. He does possess a certain talent. Thank you for allowing us to see it firsthand."

"Of course." She winked at Benedict and crossed her arms.

He gave a nervous laugh. "Ah yes, I do enjoy telling falsehoods in order to entertain others."

"Good man, good sense of humor, good man." Lord

Kerrington was still chuckling.

Benedict scooted closer to Katherine and grasped her hand hard within his.

She squeaked but otherwise made no movement.

"I have half a mind to strangle you." He felt his jaw clench in frustration.

"But, your grace?" Katherine turned her deep blue eyes toward him and whispered, "Then you would no longer be able to kiss me, and you do enjoy that, don't you?"

Before he could speak, she shushed him. "No, no, you've had quite the ordeal tonight, your grace. Pray, do not exert yourself any further. Besides, you've kissed a woman, lived through a fight and apparently a terrible bout with dust. You deserve your rest. Just remember this one thing."

"What's that?" Curse his voice for being hoarse with need.

"This round goes to me."

"Minx."

"Rogue."

"Flirt."

"Devil."

He sighed. "Agreed. I have been bested."

"Why, your grace!" Her eyelashes fluttered. He couldn't take his eyes away from her face if he wanted to. "How sporting of you."

And then, the woman, the very same one who threatened his life so many years before, managed the impossible.

She didn't sneak, but rather stomped right into his heart, threatening something much more dangerous than his life.

His absolute and utter devotion.

Devil take him, he'd be shocked if he lasted the two weeks without his heart, soul, life, and everything else he possessed on a platter before the girl.

The whole idea that she could enter into his life so

quickly and steal his very small heart made him deuced uncomfortable. She was more than a pretty face, and despite his desire to bed her, he found himself wanting to wed her. Perhaps he was going mad? It may be the only explanation as to why he continued to stop himself from fully ruining her, from making her his. Though his body ached with need, for the first time in his life, he was putting another human being before himself. It was such an odd feeling that he found he almost needed to sit before his knees buckled beneath him sending him to the floor.

What was this foreign feeling? Would it ever go away? Or was the only cure the very same girl that both provoked and enflamed him?

****

He wasn't going to last a week.

Then again, she wasn't sure she was going to last the carriage ride home. The man was altogether too large to fit in that stifling carriage.

After his aunt accidently tread on her father's foot with her cane, well, he felt a bruised foot as well as a bruised ego, no doubt.

Meaning, her parents left the opera early.

Thanking the heavens that she still had Benedict's fire-breathing aunt with them, Katherine soon realized her joy would be short-lived. When the very dragon toppled over in her chair.

"Oh, you two stay, stay! After all, you are betrothed."

"I will see that Lady Katherine reaches her home this evening," Benedict had drawled, his smirk giving way to the utter satisfaction he most likely felt with Katherine in his clutches again.

"Well, if you insist." The dowager looked to Katherine.

"I would be delighted to stay and watch the remainder of the opera with his grace."

"Well, that's settled!" The dowager nodded her head slowly. The poor thing did look quite put out, perhaps she was coming down with the ague? Which is exactly what she had suggested to Benedict.

He laughed, and stated that she was known for having a list of ailments, all of which were non-existent but always helpful in her manipulations and strategies.

They were silent the rest of the opera.

And in the carriage.

Until, all of a sudden Benedict stopped the carriage a block from her house. "You cannot be silent!"

"Why ever not?" she near shouted.

"It isn't like you!"

"Pardon?"

"Silence? Beauty? Intelligence? Devil take me, it isn't at all like you! Be disagreeable. Saints alive, help a man out! It would be so much easier to marry a woman who was...was..."

She must have hit him harder than she thought.

"Let me see if I understand you correctly. You desire for me to be undesirable."

"Thank the saints, yes!" He lifted his eyes heavenward and sighed happily. "Do you not understand? I was just getting used to the idea of being married, of being forced— nay, coerced, perhaps manipulated is a better word? Yes, manipulated—into marrying you! At least then, I knew I could keep my distance. After all, you'd probably send me to an early grave, and then I wouldn't have to suffer along side you in holy matrimony."

"How romantic."

He shrugged. He would shrug at a time like this. Devil take him.

"But now, don't you see how much more difficult it is

going to be for me to be…Well, to be…" He bit his lip and scowled.

"Selfish?" she offered.

"Yes!" he roared. "Now wait one minute, I wouldn't necessarily say it's selfish to want to live one's life without the irritation of a woman by their side."

"Your words are like poetry," she gushed mockingly.

Banbury glared. "I do not want marriage. Least of all with a woman who can throw a right punch with the best of them, nor one who I can't imagine without pigtails. Besides, she picked you."

"By she you mean the dowager? Were we not just discussing this last night? She picked me for your cousin, not you. Truly, you need to learn the art of humility."

"She tricked me," he said, ignoring her. "Besides, you're stuck with me. Forget the courting, hang it all! You will marry me, and you will be boring!"

Perhaps she should tell the footman to take them to Bedlam instead of her home. "Are you unwell?" She leaned forward and lifted a hand to his cheek.

"Why the blazes would I be well? A few days ago, I was happily drinking the night away at a gambling hell. And now, now, I'm…going to the opera with my aunt of all people! Along with my soon-to-be wife. By Jove, I'm going to have a wife…" He leaned his head back against the seat.

"And an apoplectic fit if you don't calm down," she added.

He glared. "My thanks. That was ever so helpful in putting my mood in a better state."

"I don't love you," she stated rather boldly.

He opened his eyes and burst out laughing. "Truly, a man can't hear that enough. It is akin to a woman confessing that she only has days to live and has never been with a man, or when the proprietor suddenly announces that the whiskey is free."

"You don't love me."

He paused.

Saints alive, why was he pausing?

The air in the carriage swam with tension.

"No?" The word hung as a question between them. He blinked his eyes a few times as if trying to ascertain that they were still functioning, a side effect of the dust no doubt.

"No." She nodded and leaned forward. "But, your grace. We are stuck. Let us think nothing more of crying off or trying to best one another. Can we not simply be friends?"

"Marriage and friendship?" He looked skeptical as his eyebrows drew together.

She nodded.

"I guess this means you won't try to be boring."

"I cannot be what I am not."

His eyes narrowed.

She cleared her throat and patted his hand. "Just like you cannot help but be disagreeable and grumpy with a nasty habit of forgetting to smile."

Banbury opened his mouth to speak, but she kept talking.

"And let us not forget your horrid talent at telling a fib. Gracious, my three-year-old niece could do it better. Dust? Really?"

"In my defense, I *am* allergic."

She grinned. "Remind me to bring dust to our ceremony."

"Wouldn't shock me at all if you arrived with pistols firing, let alone dust."

"It would be less than you deserve," she added.

"Minx." He tapped the roof of the carriage and sighed. "Friends?" His hand was outstretched in a manner signaling a peace of sorts. So why, when her gloved hand touched his, did she feel that she had just made a deal with the devil?

He smiled.

She gulped. Because the truth hit her full force. She didn't feel like she had made a deal with the devil. The deal was already done, and the devil looked quite pleased.

Chapter Eleven

What's a Devil to Do?

He was worse than a woman. His own mood swings were driving him mad; he could only imagine how Katherine felt, that is, if he was one to care about others' feelings, which of course, he didn't.

He was the devil after all.

It was morning, precisely two days since the dreaded ball where his life changed forever, and less than twenty-four hours since his last erotic kiss with the woman that was to be his wife. By his calculations, he had less than two weeks before the Kringle Ball. The very same ball that sealed his fate as a leg-shackled duke.

When had he lost control of his life?

Was it the day he stepped into Agatha's house? Or perhaps the very second he decided to accept her invitation?

And now, he was stuck.

With a wife he didn't want, well, that is to say he didn't emotionally want her. Wanting her physically was quite another topic entirely. His body replayed images of her responsive kiss over and over again until his only solace was whiskey.

He finished half the bottle. Not a proud moment since he wasn't one to normally drink alone.

The problem was he saw no way out of this predicament. Contrary to popular notion, he truly did possess a heart, though it was small, and at times he did wonder if it worked properly. Especially considering he rarely felt guilty for ruining women left and right. It had always been a sport, a way to pass time, an entertaining amusement.

But now, he had one woman. One irritatingly attractive woman who was depending on him to make one right decision amidst all the bad ones.

He swallowed, suddenly wishing he wasn't nursing a headache or nausea, for the whiskey called out to him again.

There was no way out of the mess.

It would be helpful if the chit would at least be agreeable. His demands were straightforward and honest, but in the end, it wouldn't have mattered if she tried to be boring. Her eyes shone with intelligence.

Nor if she tried to be indifferent, her mouth often curved into a mischievous smile when she thought nobody was watching.

But he watched.

He noticed.

Devil take him, he was actually falling for a woman who wasn't his mistress.

Which meant he was in danger of creating the biggest scandal the *ton* would ever see or talk about for centuries.

The Devil Duke was successfully becoming besotted with the very woman he was going to marry.

Wonders never ceased.

He smiled, despite a herculean effort not to and took a

slow sip of coffee.

"Your grace, this just came for you. It is urgent that you respond straight away." His butler bowed, but made no move to leave.

Benedict took the letter into his hand and broke the seal.

A house party.

Gads, he hadn't been to a house party in years.

He continued reading.

The party was to be thrown at Lord Marks' estate just outside London.

A holiday party.

His mind worked sluggishly through the details. It would be endless days filled with ice-skating and games.

It sounded like the exact opposite of something he would normally agree to.

Which was why, when he wrote his acceptance, he nearly banged his head against the table in order to conjure up part of his old self.

"Deuced idiot is what I am," he mumbled as he closed his eyes, and contemplated returning to bed.

But then a thought struck him.

A devilish thought, one that brought a cheerful smile to his face and did wonders for his headache.

Katherine.

What he needed was to put her in situations where she would yet again prove disastrous and dangerous, and would successfully kill any sort of attachment he had for her. It would remind him that she was not any type of woman he wanted to marry. This was so simple! The girl was as clumsy as she was beautiful. Put the girl in skates and she would find the thin ice.

He laughed aloud nearly scaring himself in the process, for he had just laughed over the thought of a girl falling into an ice pond.

His smile faded. Did he truly just imagine her beautiful

body falling into an icy hole? What in the blazes was wrong with him? Perhaps she could just take a tumble, reminding him again that she was not fit to be a duchess and certainly unfit to be wed.

On the other hand, considering his imagination had run away with him again, mayhap he should return to bed?

No, no, he scolded himself. He had preparations to make.

****

One day later

Katherine glared at the man sitting opposite her. The carriage hit a bump; she glared harder. Could he not feel the penetration of her stare?

"You're going to hurt me if you keep glowering at me in that fashion, or worse your eyes will be stuck in that position, and we both know how offensive you find me." He grinned, his dimples mocking her every nerve.

Drat the man! Days ago, she did not think him capable of emotion, let alone smiling! And now he was. Practically enthusiastic. When she agreed to be his friend despite having to marry him, it seemed the best course of action.

In her defense, she had thought to only see him a few more times before the Kringle Ball, and at worse, every day.

But now, she was to spend four days in his company.

In his cousin's company.

She'd be shocked if she didn't expire from the emotional turmoil of it all.

Add in ice-skating and other games, and she was a ball of nerves. It had been pure luck on her part that she had managed not to accost the duke in the past three days.

Surely her luck was running out.

Benedict grinned again. Yes, it was most definitely

running out.

"Am I to understand that you've never ice skated before?" he asked, looking idly amused. If she could call inspecting her gloves and smiling amused.

"I am quite skilled at ice skating, your grace."

He cursed aloud and leveled her with a glare so intense, she was surprised her face didn't go up in flames.

"We are to be husband and wife. I believe you can cease from calling me your grace, at least in private."

"Sorry, Benedict."

His teeth clenched. "Don't know why you'd have such trouble saying my name now, you were deuced good at screaming it when you were busy trying to plan my demise."

Katherine bit her bottom lip trying to keep from smiling. "I was concerned for your welfare."

"Concerned?" He tilted his head and leaned forward. "Pray tell, were you concerned before or after I was knocked out from a tree branch those many years ago?"

She managed a stoic face. "After."

"And when I fell off the balcony?"

"Before."

"Why before?"

"Your aunt was hunting for you that night as well, Benedict, and if memory serves, you had just wagered a thousand pounds that it would rain before morning."

Benedict's face turned serious. "How did you know my aunt was chasing me?"

"Oh, you looked quite frantic, which is why I offered you an escape."

"The escape being my ultimate death?"

"I didn't say I planned it *well*," Katherine argued. At this point, her smile was going to freeze onto her face, permanent that it was.

"Minx, you've been trying to ruin me your whole life,

admit it."

Katherine laughed. "Perhaps you're just upset that I ruined you first, Benedict." His name came out as a whisper.

Eyes darkening, he leaned forward. "I didn't know you could ruin a devil."

"And I didn't know you could redeem one, yet here we are."

"Yes." His hands moved to her shoulders and then her neck. "Here we are."

His lips were just a breath away from hers, but the carriage jolted them out of their moment, putting a stop to whatever spell had descended upon the carriage.

"I'll just be reading then," Katherine said.

"...must catch up on my sleep, you understand," he answered at the same time and quickly closed his eyes.

****

Catch up on his sleep? More like experience firsthand torture. Confound it! Benedict had again almost kissed the girl!

It wasn't necessarily the kiss that upset him.

No, it was the way his body responded to her laugh, her every word, as if she wasn't just conversing with him but making love to him.

Which was sheer madness! Speaking was not making love.

And yet, with Katherine it was.

Every word formed with her delicate lips, every sigh that escaped without her notice, every bat of her lashes.

Mad. He was going absolutely mad.

But kissing her? It would make things exponentially worse, for he wouldn't stop at one kiss. He would not insult his own intelligence by justifying such an action.

With Katherine, a kiss had never been a kiss, but sheer ecstasy like he had never known. Her smell, her taste, everything about her unique and spiced.

Better than whiskey. Blast, better than sex.

Madness. When a man compared kissing to sex and kissing won out, he needed to embark on a weeklong stint of debauchery.

Yet, all he could think about was her kiss, her lips, and the simple idea that in a few short weeks she would say yes, and he could spend his days and his nights finding out what was so intriguing about the saucy minx sitting in that carriage.

Yet, a part, a small part, warned him that once he began that discovery, he would never want to stop.

Chapter Twelve

A Snowball For A Duke

Katherine was jolted awake by Benedict's hand.

"Well? Are you going to wake up, or do I need to carry you?"

Ah, just what she needed—a reminder of why he was called the Devil Duke, why he was disagreeable, and why she was upset she wasn't with his cousin. Katherine had needed that reminder, for her heart had felt lost on the journey, and she wasn't sure what was happening to her. Something larger than friendship was blossoming between them.

And she wasn't sure her heart could take the devastation of what a man like Benedict would bring. Surely she could marry him and keep herself indifferent if he was disagreeable. But what if she began to like him, to befriend him, to love him?

He would destroy her.

It would start slow. Most likely Benedict would show her firsthand exactly why women whispered about his sexual encounters. But after a few weeks or even a few months, he would get bored. His eyes would wander in the general direction of the courtesans, and he would be lost forever.

His laugh, gone.

His smile, non-existent.

And she would be heartbroken.

Which was why, when he woke her up with a smile on his face, she nudged him out of the way and stepped out of the carriage on her own.

What she didn't know was that the ground was far closer than she realized, and she nearly lost her footing.

Thankfully, Benedict was close behind her and caught her arm, but not before it hit him square in the face with a resounding thud.

The footmen gasped.

But Katherine laughed.

Benedict cursed. "And there she is. I was wondering when your clumsy self was to make another appearance."

She curtsied, because really there was nothing else to do in such circumstances, and wonder of all wonders the Devil Duke laughed heartily, causing the footmen to gasp for an entirely different reason.

Naturally his laugh was followed by an excessive amount of throat clearing and chest thumping. After all, the devil was to never laugh in public. Benedict had always tried to keep his manners indifferent when in the presence of the *ton*, far be it from them to discover he actually had a heart. The mamas would be relentless in their pursuit if they thought him anything but disagreeable.

Katherine wasn't sure what possessed her to indulge the man in a bit of playfulness. Maybe it was the way he cloaked his merriment with a devil-may-care attitude, or the line of his shoulders when he brought them back and tried to escort her into the large house.

Perhaps, she thought as she looped her arms within his,

childhood never truly leaves you. Maybe your physical body grows into what society deems acceptable, but those dreams, the itches you get to do something adventurous and dangerous never die. If anything, they are more intense in their drive, for the minute you decide to give in to the immaturity that plagued you when you were small, you are able to be free, to laugh, and to fly.

"Benedict," she whispered out of earshot of the footman. No doubt they would expire on the spot if they heard her addressing him as such.

"Hmm?" He turned his large body toward hers. Eyebrows drawn in as if he was contemplating the meaning of life.

"I'm sorry."

"Sorry? Whatever for?"

With a quick tug, she had him on his back against the snowy powder of the ground.

"What the devil!" he shouted.

And then Katherine grabbed a touch of snow in her hand and drizzled it on his face as if it were sand.

He was very serious then.

Almost too serious.

Making her think she had finally gone too far.

And then with a roar, he jumped to his feet firmly packing a snowball in his hand as his eyes turned to steel. "Run."

So she did.

As fast as her legs could carry her, she ran around the outside of the estate laughing the whole way. Snowballs flew past her head. Giggling, she found it nearly impossible to keep running as she heard him yelling threats from behind.

And then his large arms came around her, and he whispered hoarsely in her ear, "Now, it's my turn to be sorry."

"For wh—"

Benedict pushed her to the ground and pounced near her

in the snow, he pinned her to the cold wet earth and leaned in. Panting, he lifted the snowball in his hand and laughed. "What will you give me for a truce, my lady?"

Giggling, she pushed the escaped hair away from her face and gazed into his eyes. It felt quite like she was falling, only she was nowhere near a cliff or in danger. Yet his heart screamed *jump, jump, jump*. "Will a kiss be acceptable?"

"No." He threw the snowball down to the ground.

Her heart thudded in her chest to a near stop.

Benedict's hands threaded through her hair pulling her head closer to his until their breaths were mingled. "Just one kiss is never acceptable."

At the first touch of their lips, she felt her world spin. His kiss was playful, as his tongue wrestled with hers and then slid out of her mouth. He tilted his head at a different angle, his cold nose lighting her skin like a fire, and then warmth met her again, as he tugged her head tighter and pressed his lips harder until it was difficult to breathe.

"One kiss is never acceptable," he repeated out of breath and held out his hand. Unashamed, and still flushed from their little game, she took his arm and walked with him back to the front of the house.

"I fear we've caused a bigger scandal than when the *ton* saw my knees," she said changing the subject—anything to rid herself of the odd tingling sensation Benedict's mouth had left on her person.

Benedict pulled her closer and kissed the top of her head. "I'm a duke. Believe me, the footmen will be silent, and as for everyone else, it appears we are the first to arrive."

"But what about Lord Marks? Surely he'll see the state of our dress?" She looked into his eyes and tried to calm her breathing. Breathtakingly handsome, he merely shrugged. "That part, I already have figured out."

"What do you mean?" Katherine asked.

"You'll see."

Fifteen minutes later, standing in front of the fire in her room, she knew exactly what the devil had meant. For the second Lord Marks had greeted them, Benedict had gone into detail of how Katherine, in all her clumsiness, had tripped him, causing them both to fall into the snow. He added that she often fell and took others with her, so it would be wise to watch his footing throughout the week. And then he winked.

"I should have known," she said before they parted ways to their rooms.

"But of course, my dear. You know how I love telling falsehoods."

"Touché."

"Does this mean I win this round?" He brought her hand to his lips and kissed each knuckle. His eyes danced with merriment as he licked his lips.

"Yes."

"Then, I believe we're even. Now change out of those clothes before you catch a chill. After all, I cannot in good sport play a game with someone who's ill."

She withdrew her hand and curtsied but not before rolling her eyes at the handsome man. He paused, focusing on her lips and then her eyes.

"Minx."

"Rogue."

"I shall see you at dinner."

"You shall."

And again they paused, words left unsaid. But weren't actions louder than words, for their very actions must have led everyone to believe that a minute without one another was like a thousand deaths, and so Katherine was the first to turn on her heel and enter her chambers.

She smiled at the memory of the day then cursed herself for being so infatuated. All was lost, for he already had the better part of her heart.

"Please don't break it," she whispered into the fire and closed her eyes as her chest constricted with that all too familiar pain of rejection. Benedict never said he wanted her, and it was clear that Paisley had still thought her a little girl. Fear squeezed the walls of her throat threatening to close it all together. Was he toying with her? Or did he truly enjoy their flirtation? And if he did, was it enough for him to marry her in earnest?

The flames licked into the air as if mocking her. The very flames that the Devil Duke was born out of no doubt, yet a small part of him it seemed was not the man he wanted everyone to believe he was. The more moments they had together, the closer she was to understanding the man behind all the rumors.

He was actually fun.

Invigorating.

Beautiful.

She cursed. A decision needed to be made. Her heart was already lost, her body his. So, it was without pause that Katherine decided on giving in to the very thing she as most afraid of. If he denied her, refused to repay her vulnerability with his own truth, then at least she tried and would have no regrets, save the absolute horror of falling without the proof that he would be there to catch her.

Chapter Thirteen

Erotic Dinners and the Like

The evening of the first day of the house party was upon them, and already Benedict was feeling lost.

A snowball fight? Whatever had he been thinking? Or her for that matter! Then again, he hadn't remembered a time since he was a boy that he'd laughed so hard, or felt freer.

It was her fault.

She even turned her clumsiness into a private joke between the two, smiling at him, making him feel warm inside as if her smile held the secret to the sun's rays.

The secret to the sun's rays?

And apparently, in his mad state, he was turning into a poet.

Heaven help him.

He was losing not only his sanity but also his heart. Benedict could only hope that Katherine would do something, anything to make him remember the girl she once was, not the seductive woman he currently saw.

It had taken the power of God alone to get him to stop kissing her in the snow and the strength of angels to push his feet toward the house.

He made his way down the stairs to the dining room and cursed his eyes for scanning the room in hopes to see Katherine.

She was nowhere to be seen.

Perplexed, he didn't even see Lord Marks until the man cleared his throat. "Say, I'm not sure I've ever seen you so distracted, your grace."

"Yes well, I..." Benedict felt off balance, as if someone had pushed him onto ice without skates. "Have an aversion to cold weather," he offered, wanting to slap himself for such a ridiculous excuse.

"Do you now?" Lord Marks looked amused, his brown eyes twinkling as he folded his arms across his chest.

"Yes." Benedict stood his ground and promptly began to sweat. He still felt odd as if something was off, perhaps the universe was trying to communicate with him that he needed to stop being a besotted fool and kissing girls who would rather fillet him alive than marry him. And then, his eyes again scanned the doors to the dining room. They opened.

His mouth dropped open.

Lord Marks cleared his throat. "Close your mouth before you scare the poor thing. She is not to be the meal."

Saints alive, let her at least be the dessert then.

Katherine walked in with more grace than she ought to possess considering she had only hours ago tripped out of the carriage and started the most arousing snowball fight he had ever had the pleasure of participating in.

His eyes openly admired her form in the blue dinner dress. Had she any idea how much skin she was showing? The poor thing was going to freeze to death! Suddenly irate and irritated that she would think nothing of her health, Benedict stomped over to where she stood and grabbed her arm roughly, placing it within his and growled.

Yes, like a dog. He growled to show his displeasure. Was he now at odds with his body? It seemed to instinctively do things it ought not do. Poetry? Growling? Staring? Salivating? Sweating?

Cursing, he clenched her hand and gave her a tight smile. "Beautiful dress."

"Why thank you I—"

"—where would the rest of it be? Hmm?" His eyes flickered to her breasts and then back up to her face, and to his ultimate shame, back down to her breasts where they stayed for a painfully long time until she nudged him in the ribs.

"Manners, you devil." Katherine winked.

His stomach did an odd sort of flop.

His heart increased his blood flow to all the wrong areas of anatomy, and when he made introductions to the rest of the dinner party, he felt such a stab of jealousy when Sir Constantine's gaze flew to her bosom that he thought his head would explode.

If not for Katherine being on his arm, he would have ripped the man's head off and beat him with it. But the minute he tensed, Katherine looked up through dark lashes and smiled brilliantly, striking him dumb and immobile.

"Shall we sit?" she whispered, her lips only inches from his.

Why did her simple invitation seem to be one of sin rather than common sense? *Shall we sit?* Why the devil would he sit when he wanted nothing more than to lay, plunder, possess…Truly he could think of any number of actions he would rather give his full participation to than sitting.

Alas, he was in public, and though his reputation laughed in the face of propriety, he couldn't bring himself to ravish the girl in public, no matter how badly he desired it. Katherine's eyes crinkled at the sides as she offered a small smile and brought her hand down her neck to her chest.

Minx.

Dessert, yes she would be his dessert if he made it through dinner, but he had his doubts.

By the time the third course was served, Benedict had imagined all sorts of ways to kill oneself with a fork.

There was of course, the slow death of pounding one's head against the sharp object. Naturally, he could slice his skin with the knife if he felt so compelled. And his personal favorite, try to swallow the thing and hope death would come swiftly in the form of asphyxiation.

None of those options, however, provided him a fast enough escape from his current predicament.

It had all started with the soup.

And went downhill from there.

There was nothing particularly wrong with the soup. It was hot, and he was hungry, but his blasted eye had the ridiculous notion that it needed to pay attention to the woman on his right.

Katherine, to be exact.

And blast if that eye didn't train on her very lips as she held the spoon near them and closed her eyes in ecstasy.

He had shifted in his chair.

Deuced uncomfortable dinner to be honest.

He prayed the soup would be taken away and fifteen agonizing minutes later, it was replaced with something new.

Ah! Yes, at least roast goose would give him respite. For what woman in all creation could make roast goose look erotic?

Oh, how wrong he had been.

Even now his body tightened at the thought.

And he wasn't quite sure eating dinner would ever be enjoyable again, at least not when he had guests surrounding him and Katherine dropping pieces of meat into her delicate mouth. He nearly wept as she would close her eyes and moan when no one was looking, no one but him unfortunately. Her vulgarity knew no end, yet he found it fascinating as the low rumble would start in her throat and spread until he nearly dropped his fork each time she brought food to her lips. Finally, she would swallow and take a sip of wine, what he wouldn't give to be glassware in that moment.

Well, he hadn't eaten anything at all, which of course caused a ridiculous amount of questions. Was he feeling well? Had the ride from town been rough? *If only*, he thought, *if only it was anything but demure.*

Voice hoarse, he had merely shook his head and prayed for Katherine to spill her wine or do something clumsy.

Instead, his unsteady hand hit the wine causing a fiasco at the table. Once dessert was served, the women retired away from the men, and he was finally at peace with his cheroot and brandy out on the balcony.

And then he felt her.

Benedict couldn't help but think it had to be some sort of sixth sense, that every time she was near, he would begin to shake and lose control of his calm exterior. His body would heat, thinking on her until he wanted to begin stripping his clothes.

"Am I interrupting?" she asked, lightly falling beside him, her dainty arms leaned across the balcony, breasts spilled over her dress, and again he was struck dumb. Why the blazes hadn't she worn a coat?

"You'll catch your death out here," he grumbled, disgusted with his lack of bodily control. As it was, he was having a devil of a time keeping his arousal in check, and he hadn't even touched the girl.

"Well, good thing I have my *fiancé* nearby to warm me up." Katherine looked up at him with merry eyes and patted him lightly on the shoulder.

It was his undoing.

That one touch.

The one gaze from her eyes.

And again he found himself falling, as if he could no longer see straight or stay in balance if his life depended on it. His need was so great that he wanted to yell and laugh at the same time.

Instead he just kissed her.

But to say it was just a kiss would be like saying the ocean was just a mass of water, or the sun was just a star. No, this kiss was unlike any other kiss he had ever experienced in his lifetime or hoped to experience.

Because, he thought as his lips danced with hers, it was shared with his other half.

And in that kiss, as she sighed into his arms, as his tongue dove deep into the velvet moisture of her mouth, he knew he wanted to continue to fall if it meant she would be the one to catch him.

In the end, is that not what everyone else wanted?

With the strength of a god, he pulled back and muffled a curse before raising his eyes heavenward. "She's won, by Jove, she's won."

"Pardon?" Katherine's lips were still swollen from their kiss, her eyes barely visible through her thick lashes. "Who won?"

"The devil."

"I thought you were the devil?"

He snickered. "Where did you think I descended from? Thin air? And I was referring to my aunt."

"Oh?" Katherine squinted at him as if he had in fact turned into a pink unicorn. To be fair, he was acting like a complete idiot, spouting nonsense into the sky like a fool. He sighed and pinched the bridge of his nose.

"Are you well?" she whispered near his face, too near, for it caused him to jerk back and trip. He hadn't the grace or common sense to break his fall as he collapsed onto the hard ground and looked up into her amused eyes.

Gracefully, she knelt down and felt his head. "You're positively flushed, shall I take you to bed?"

"Please." He begged, wanting much more than she was offering, innocent that she was.

"I meant," she scolded, hitting him with her hand, "should I help you to you room then promptly leave you to suffer alone?"

Well, at least she didn't offer to kill him. He had been quite forward with her all evening, and he deduced he was already on some sort of borrowed time considering his behavior was appalling. Not that he wasn't used to offending others, but not her.

Not her.

Suddenly, he wanted much more than to give in because his aunt desired him to marry.

He wanted to.

Devil take him...he wanted to treat her...

Why was it so hard to say in his head?

He wanted to court the girl, to do right by her.

He waved in the air, literally lifted his hand and waved, as all of his best laid plans flew into the night sky. There would be no ravishing, no ruining, no laughing in the face of marriage.

No, he imagined he was the type of man that once marriage took him prisoner, he would happily, if not drunkenly, offer his leg willingly to the ball and chain and boast about it for the rest of his days.

Such a nuisance that.

Having forgot that he waved into the night sky, Katherine felt his forehead again. "You do not feel feverish. Tell me, what is your name, and where are you?"

Oh, he could have fun with this one. Perhaps just a little ruin never hurt anyone? He gave a goofy grin and shrugged.

"Oh my!" Katherine helped him to his feet and immediately began reprimanding him as she led him into the house. "And to think you would get so foxed! My goodness, have you any care for your reputation? Never mind I momentarily forgot with whom I was speaking. But we both know how accident-prone you can be. Imagine if you would have fallen from the balcony! Whatever would we do!"

He smiled smugly. Of course she cared for his welfare. It felt good.

"I mean..." She cursed under her breath. "Imagine the mess the servants would have to clean up, and then I would have to tell your dragon of an aunt that I led you to your death, and she would most likely say *finally*, considering I have brought you quite close at least three times."

"Four." He coughed then slapped the silly grin back in place.

Her eyes narrowed.

He purposefully tripped on the first stair.

Shaking her head, she helped him up the stairs and continued her tirade until she pushed open the bedroom doors and laid him across the bed.

Surely in his drunken, albeit falsely drunken, state one could not blame him for taking full advantage.

And take full advantage he did. With a sigh he pulled her onto his body and closed his eyes.

Chapter Fourteen

Seduction by Moonlight

"*Oomph!*" Katherine fell across his hard muscled body with a thud. Well, now he'd done it. She was in somewhat of a pickle. How the devil was she to pry her body from his when the man's hands were pulling her tighter and tighter against him?

Honestly, she'd never seen him so foxed before. Was he that upset over the marriage? Perhaps, it was boredom. He was, after all, the devil. Meaning he was used to much more lively entertainment than eating a casual dinner and smoking a cheroot.

She sighed and tried to pry her body free.

Benedict's response was a moan. His lips somehow found hers again and he worked his spell, his wicked magic over her body until she was sure she was going to go to a very fiery place.

They were not married.

They were only betrothed.

Accidently, of course.

And now she was in his bedroom, his bedroom! Acting the absolute wanton, but oh the things he did with his tongue.

"Benedict," she whispered against his lips. "Benedict, you must let me go."

"No."

"No?" His lips moved to her neck, his warm tongue traced the curve of her jaw.

Oh the wicked things he did with his tongue. "Yes, you want me to let you go, or no, you want to stay?"

"Yes, no!"

"Wait, do you mean yes or no? Sorry love, I'm somewhat foxed and need you to be a little more direct."

She kicked him with her foot.

He laughed. "I deserved that. It appears when I asked for you to be direct, you were under the impression I wanted violence."

Katherine closed her eyes and leaned her forehead against his. "You are impossible."

"So I've been told." He sighed and then miraculously released her. Only, she wasn't prepared so she fell off the bed and landed with a thud on the floor.

Benedict chuckled then peeked over the edge. "Take a tumble, did you?"

"Sometimes I wish I could slap you."

"Believe me, love, it would only encourage me more."

She smiled despite herself and righted her skirts so she wasn't again flashing her knees to the duke and stood on wobbly legs.

"Goodnight, your grace," she said in her haughtiest voice.

"Goodnight, my love."

Rolling her eyes, she walked to the door. He was most definitely foxed, for everyone knew the Devil Duke did not love. He was more likely to jump off the highest balcony in London than admit any sort of emotional attachment.

This really was a pity, considering her heart did a tiny clench when he uttered those sacred words.

"Goodnight," she said again before stepping quietly into the hall.

****

Katherine was slow to rise. By the time she made it down to break her fast, nearly all the guests were already seated and eating.

She took a plate and began to fill it.

As she reached for the toast, a hand slipped beneath hers and took the plate away. "Allow me."

She looked up and nearly fainted dead away. The duke of Paisley began filling her plate with every available dish, all the while glaring at her as if she had suddenly announced that she was fighting for Napoleon.

"Thank you?" she said trying to take the plate from his hands.

"What the devil did you do?" he seethed.

"Pardon?"

"You heard me." His Scottish brogue was fighting to break through the words. "Last I left my cousin, he was debauching the better half of London and after nearly a week in your presence and he's, he's…well, look at him."

Perplexed, she looked in the direction that Baldwyn pointed. Benedict was sitting at the table, conversing with everyone around him and laughing. Everything looked as it should. Perhaps Paisley was the one with the issue, was he foxed this early?

She turned back to the Scottish duke. "I have no idea what you're referring to. He's acting perfectly fine." She shrugged and continued piling food onto her plate.

"Fine!" Paisley roared, gaining attention from everyone in the room including Benedict whose smile very quickly faded as he pushed away from the table, his chair scraping the floor. "Drinking, scowling, prowling, devil take it! Stripping naked in public! Those are the things I come to expect from my cousin, not this…this lightheartedness! I want him back. Give him back."

"Give what back?" Benedict interrupted.

"Good morning, your grace. It seems your cousin would like me to give back your scowl, prowl, drink, and what else? Oh yes, he would prefer if you were naked."

Paisley blushed. "That is *not* what I meant."

"Wasn't it?" Katherine winked.

"It's just…Benedict." He turned to his cousin. "Why the devil are you so happy? It's as if she's won." At Benedict's sheepish look Paisley cursed fluently. "Don't tell me. Do not tell me. You, you, you…"

"Use your words." Benedict slapped him on the back.

"Y-you are happily marching to the marriage drum! And with her!" He pointed at Katherine. Honestly, was she so bad?

"Yes." Benedict turned to her and grabbed her hand placing a kiss across the knuckles. "*Her*."

Well, that was nice. With a smug grin, she glanced back to Paisley and lifted an eyebrow.

"I cannot believe this." Paisley shook his head. "I…I…"

"Your grace?" Katherine tilted her head. "You wouldn't be afraid of the same fate, now would you?"

"Ha, ha!" He laughed and slapped his leg. "Now, that is, absolutely ridic—"

He froze, the words died on his lips. His eyes glazed over, Katherine fought the urge to wave in front of his face. Instead, she looked in the direction that Baldwyn was focused on. Lady Anastasia entered the room, looking much like a fairy princess. That was when Katherine knew. The poor man had already fallen. He just didn't know what to do about it.

"Go." Katherine pushed him. "Tell her she looks pretty."

"What?" he scoffed.

"Try kissing her hand," Benedict offered. "And do attempt to keep the drool from dribbling out of your mouth."

With that, they both pushed him in her direction and sighed in unison.

After a few minutes, Katherine felt Benedict's hand on her back, and then his lips near her ear. "Ice skating?"

"Yes."

A loud commotion at the door interrupted their moment.

Suddenly servants were rushing out of the dining room.

And then running.

Several stopped and began to mumble prayers.

Were they under attack?

Had something happened?

"Hurry!" the butler yelled, then stopped and pulled out a handkerchief and wiped his perspiring face. "It must be perfect!"

A footman quickly opened a flask and gulped its contents. Another began to cry.

What the devil?

And then she heard it.

But she was convinced rather than hearing the familiar female shrieking, Benedict *felt* her presence.

"Am I too late to join the party?"

The voice was unmistakable. In fact, it seemed the entire room went tight with tension and mumbled under their breath in unison, "Agatha."

Chapter Fifteen

The Visitation

Benedict suddenly wished lightning would strike the very ground he stood on. Logically speaking that is, he would push Katherine out of the way and take the brunt of it. Then again, she would be left to face Agatha without him.

Sometimes it was better to be the selfish cur.

Struggling between his two lofty dreams, Benedict decided it was time to face the music, or in this case the dragon, and stood his ground, pulling Katherine firmly by his side.

Agatha hobbled in, rather than walked. It seemed her health truly had taken a decline. Either that or she was a splendid actress and belonged on Drury Lane with the rest of them.

Most likely the latter.

"Ah, Aunt! How splendid to see you!" The lie fell easily off his lips as did his smile, stunning his aunt so completely that her jaw dropped and a smile tugged at the corners of her mouth.

"I knew it!" she shouted. Did she need to shout her victory in front of an audience?

"Knew what?" Katherine asked.

"That he would one day remember to smile. He just needed something to smile about. Isn't that right, my dear?"

Katherine blushed profusely.

"Am I interrupting the morning meal?" Agatha peered around Benedict to see everyone sitting stiffly at the table.

"Not at all, Aunt. Join us?" He held out his hand as a sort of peace offering.

Grinning, she took it and tucked his arm close to her frail body. Had she been losing weight? She smelt of his family, of memories, and he was suddenly feeling like an absolute cad for his treatment of her, his one remaining relative.

"Do tell me you shall go ice-skating on the pond?" Her eyes glistened.

"Yes," he answered unable to pull his gaze away from her face. When did she begin to age? And why was her skin so pale?

Katherine joined them and kissed Agatha on the cheek. He never thought he'd see the day that his aunt would blush. "Actually, would you care to join us? We were just going to grab our skates."

Agatha smiled and patted Katherine's hand. "I would love to, dear."

Dear? Benedict fought to keep the shock from his face.

"It is such a beautiful house, and a perfect day for the outdoors!" Agatha announced. At that precise moment, the butler collapsed and a footman exhaled thanks to God while servants slumped against the walls. As if the woman had just declared that Parliament was in session and everything was as it should be.

She gave a jolly laugh and walked out with Katherine. Benedict followed, his heart warming at Agatha and the woman he cared for chatting about ice-skating.

Chapter Sixteen

Dukes on Thin Ice

Katherine held Agatha's hand and placed it on her arm until they reached the frozen pond. After setting the dowager on a bench and wrapping her frail body in blankets, Katherine was shooed away to join the festivities.

Benedict wasn't far behind. Paisley and Lady Anastasia soon followed. Several couples were already skating on the pond, and Katherine didn't want to wait to join in the fun.

Quickly, she attached her skates, and began to wobble along. Everything was going perfectly well until the ice seemed to jump up and catch her skate, causing her to stumble. Soon her arms were waving frantically, and she could already feel the pain slicing her bottom if she were to fall.

Strong arms surrounded her, and then warm breath grazed her ear. "May I be of assistance, my lady?"

Katherine regained her balance and looked at her rescuer.

The joke was obviously on her, for God hadn't sent her a guardian angel. No, something quite the opposite.

If anything, Benedict's devilishly handsome looks seemed to only intensify with the white snow in the background. Curse the man.

"My thanks." She smiled.

He held out his arm. With a laugh, she tucked her arm within his and skated alongside him. They pulled up right next to Paisley and Lady Anastasia.

"Paisley, you skate like a woman," Benedict called out in good humor then nudged Katherine. "Looks like one, too, with the way his skates are tied on. Poor soul would be better off sitting on the bench, I fear."

Katherine stifled a giggle while Paisley accepted Benedict's challenge to race.

Apparently, he felt he was defending not only his own honor but that of his *fiancée's* for he asked to carry her colors. As if he were a knight set about to joust in the tournament.

Benedict rolled his eyes and released his hold on Katherine. Her arm suddenly felt cold. Why hadn't Benedict made a similar offer? Sighing, she took a seat on the bench next to Lady Anastasia and tried not to slump or do anything to outwardly show her displeasure, though she was slightly disappointed. And then Paisley turned his beautiful eyes toward her. "Lady Katherine, might I wear yours as well?"

His mouth widened into a breathtaking smile. By Jove, she had forgotten how handsome he was! Yet, her reaction wasn't the familiar fluttering that she was so used to with Benedict. If anything it was amusement, not attraction. Odd? With a relaxed giggle, she offered a handkerchief as well, smugly satisfied as Benedict's face seemed to contort with jealousy. Serves him right for ignoring her. Well, what could she expect when a man such as he was faced with competition?

The race was fast.

Paisley was faster.

But unfortunately, Benedict was slow, though it could have been in part to the fact that Baldwyn tried to trip him around the first circle nearly sending the Devil face first onto the icy surface.

Never had she heard so many curses and oaths during a children's game.

By the time both men returned, they were breathing heavily and slapping one another on the back.

"A pleasure as always, your grace-less." Paisley smirked.

Benedict's eyes glowered, his usual mask of anger, until a small smile began to tug at his lips. Katherine knew that smile. It held secrets and manipulations. Oddly enough, it looked exactly like the smile the old dowager had when she was planning on doing something malicious. Not that she would ever tell Benedict this, for fear that he would stop smiling altogether.

"Speaking of graceless, did any of you happen to hear that commotion out in the corridor last evening?"

To say the conversation took a definite change into uncomfortable territory would be an understatement. Paisley laughed off the noise as if a vase had fallen, and Lady Anastasia looking so mortified she might have been ready to go up in flames despite the low temperatures.

A change in subject was needed.

But before Katherine could open her mouth, Lady Anastasia requested some mulled cider, successfully pulling Baldwyn away from the group, but not without giving Katherine a chilly stare.

"Care to skate, Kate?" Benedict held out his hand.

Katherine rolled her eyes. "Promise to behave?"

"I'm not sure I understand the definition of the word."

"Promise?"

"No, behave." He smirked and tugged her body so close to his she began to perspire.

"I imagine there are many words you lack the experience of hearing. Take for example—"

"—Tsk, tsk, Katherine, don't go spoiling our little outing, not after I've been watching the wind pick up your skirts enough to glance at your ankles. Think of the terrible mood you'll put me in when you begin to repeat all the words I so despise hearing."

"As in?"

"*No.* I despise the word no. It is so final, so cruel."

Katherine laughed. Oh, the man was ridiculous. "And when was the last time someone told you no, Benedict? If ever?"

"Well, I recall a certain someone saying no to my proposal, and a certain someone also saying no to courting me, which I'm still terribly distraught over. To think I missed any chances I would have had at being skillfully wooed by a woman."

"My heart aches for your loss, your grace."

"Does it?" He stopped skating, and pulled her flush against his body. "And what, do you think would cause it to beat, just a bit faster? Perhaps a kiss? Or mayhap, a tiny taste, right here I think." His hand reached out and touched her chin. "I find myself fascinated with your skin here, maybe your heart shall begin to heal if I kiss right here."

"Or..." Katherine pulled away from him, feeling flirtatious. "I'll merely say the word you despise the most in all of the world, sending you into fits of hysteria."

"Wouldn't be the first time you've caused mental and physical harm."

"And dare I say it won't be the last." She winked.

Benedict threw his head back and laughed. It seemed to silence the skating around him, causing stares to come from every direction. Suddenly uncomfortable, Katherine blushed and darted next to his side. But he wasn't totally balanced, he took a topple so hard that her own bum hurt.

Letting out a string of curses, he looked up at her from the ice and grimaced.

Katherine tried to keep from laughing. Really she did, but the look on his face was so pouty, she couldn't help but outright laugh at the picture he gave. Benedict's brows drew together, his lips forming a grimace and his face reddened just slightly.

"Very funny," he hissed through his teeth as he tried to set himself to rights. With Katherine's help they were able to slowly make their way back to the bench where Lady Anastasia and Paisley stood, mulled cider in hand.

Once Benedict was safely on the bench, he smiled and refused to release Katherine's hand. "How about a kiss for the wounded hero?"

"Wounded? Hero? Where, your grace? All I see is the devil being brought back down to earth."

Paisley burst out laughing, then at Benedict's piercing gaze, found his mulled cider even more fascinating than before.

"Please?" Benedict pulled her closer, but at that precise moment her skate caught on a chunk of ice. It felt as if her body was in slow motion, her arms flailing at her sides and then with a grimace she fell, but didn't touch the cold hard ice as she thought would happen.

Instead she was in the arms of the duke. Again.

The wrong duke. Paisley.

Mulled cider had spilt all over his clothes, but he didn't seem to care a whit. "Are you well, my lady?"

She gulped and nodded her head. "Yes, apologies. I didn't mean to ruin your cider."

"It's the cup I'm more concerned about." He looked down to the broken mug lying across the ice.

"Sorry." Shaking off the embarrassment of nearly taking

another man down with her, Katherine tried to pull away, but Paisley kept his hand firmly grasped around her waist. "On that note, I believe it is time for us to skate." He flashed her a smile and tugged her into the line of graceful skaters.

It felt different holding his hand.

As if they were opposites trying to attract one another. It was warm and comforting but nothing more.

There was no nervousness at being near Paisley, no tension as there was with Benedict.

Perplexed she looked up at his face and squinted, perhaps getting too close, for he suddenly stopped and looked at her as if she had lost her mind.

"Did you hit your head?" he asked politely.

"No." Katherine blushed. "I was merely, er, examining you."

"For?" He lifted an eyebrow.

"Imperfections?" she offered.

"And the consensus?"

"None."

Paisley put a hand to his heart and sighed. "Imagine my relief."

Katherine bit her lip. "I'm terribly sorry. It was rude of me to examine you so closely, it's just that…"

"What?"

They continued skating in circles, lazily falling behind the groups racing around and around.

"I used to have a frightful tender for you."

That stopped him. Perhaps she'd said too much.

"And now?"

"Now?" She lifted an eyebrow amused that his smirk didn't seem the least bit offended or wounded. "Now, I find you perfectly perfect."

"Yet perfectly wrong for you?"

"Absolutely. So glad you understand, Paisley."

He rolled his eyes. "Far be it from you to use any sort of propriety with a man you find so repulsive."

"Not repulsive." Katherine nudged him. "More brotherly than anything."

"Music to every man's ears." He laughed aloud, this time stopping in order to catch his breath. "And dare I guess where your affections lie?"

It was Katherine's turn to blush. But Paisley stopped her, his hand cupping her chin in an intimate yet brotherly fashion. "Do me a favor. Considering you find me perfectly brotherly, take my advice. Tread carefully with my cousin, alright?"

She nodded, and they continued to skate, falling into easy conversation and laughing the entire time.

Chapter Seventeen

A Plan Forms

Benedict watched, perplexed how his plan could go so utterly awry. His brilliance was in fact not so brilliant when his ploy of being injured left him alone on the bench pouting, and Katherine skating with his cousin.

The same cousin she used to desire.

The more they talked and laughed, the angrier he became until a soft sigh on his left stole his attention.

Lady Anastasia looked quite ill. "Are you well, Lady Anastasia?"

She sighed even deeper. "I'm lovely, just lovely," came her dry reply. If he didn't know any better, he would think she was being sarcastic.

He reached out and touched her arm. "You are quite pale." Perhaps she would take the hint and tell him why she looked so troubled. If anything it would take his mind off of shooting his cousin in the arm for touching Katherine.

"Am I?" She slumped. Never had he seen Lady Anastasia

slump as if totally defeated. "Perhaps if your grace is recovered enough, might you consider taking a turn with me around the pond? I believe the cold is settling into my bones."

A conundrum. If he skated, Katherine would know he wasn't injured, but anything was better than sitting, so he hobbled along with Lady Anastasia and pasted a smile on his face, though he could have sworn it felt menacing.

What the devil did Baldwyn find so amusing about Katherine? And why was she leaning in to him like that?

He took Lady Anastasia's outstretched hand into his, and limped while trying to appear a graceful skater, around the outer perimeter of the pond.

"Careful," Lady Anastasia said to his left. "Or you'll fall on your injury." Her smirk told him she didn't believe for one second he was injured.

"What gave me away?"

"You were limping on the other foot not five minutes ago."

Benedict cursed. "Perhaps I have a small desire to be nurtured. Is that so wrong?"

"So even the Devil desires good deeds? Interesting."

Well, when she put it that way...

"How are things progressing with my cousin?" Benedict asked politely.

A blush crept up Lady Anastasia's cheeks as she jerked her attention away from staring at Baldwyn. "I'm afraid, they aren't."

"Aren't?"

"Progressing. In fact things seem exactly the same as before, well, I guess that isn't entirely true after last night's..." She clamped her mouth shut.

Benedict laughed heartily. "Your secret's safe with me, though I wonder why the blasted man needed to be so inebriated to do something he's been craving to do for days."

"I doubt that." Lady Anastasia looked down and stopped skating.

Benedict wanted to strangle his cousin. How dare he make this woman feel unwanted? It was safe to say that if it was him the girl would already be ruined.

Katherine was a shining example of the way Benedict handled women. But this was different, so he reached over and touched her face, careful to slow his movements enough to gain attention.

"W-what are you doing?" Lady Anastasia sputtered.

"Giving you progression, my lady, in the basest way I can."

"How?"

"Jealousy." And with that Benedict leaned down to whisper nonsense into her ear about laughing and managing a tiny blush.

The timing was perfect. Baldwyn's head snapped to attention, and Katherine's eyes narrowed. Benedict shook his head slightly and Katherine nodded. How was it that by that simple action, he knew Katherine trusted him? In that very moment?

He was about to skate to her, to steal her away from his Scottish cousin, when shouting commenced from the bench.

"I want to skate, and I'm going to skate!" Agatha wailed.

Merciful heavens above, was it too much to ask for God to have at least given her a quieter voice? Or perhaps the ability to practice patience?

"Crazy old woman," he muttered as he deposited Lady Anastasia on the bench and made his way toward his aunt, praying a cloak of invisibility would suddenly find a way to shield him from her pensive glare.

She yelled again, "Gentlemen!"

Benedict swallowed. She was referring to him and Baldwyn, like little boys being punished, they slowly skated to her side, each taking an arm.

"I wish to skate," she announced.

Benedict rolled his eyes at Baldwyn who looked ready to cut himself a tiny ice hole and jump into it. "Yes, I believe the entire pond has been made aware of your desire to skate, Aunt."

"*Hmph.*" Her usual response.

"Don't argue with me, Benedict. Take my arm," she demanded. "Baldwyn! Look alive there, boy! I'm not growing any younger."

Clearly, thought Benedict.

"Take my arm and let's be off!" She waved wildly in the air as if they were planning on flying rather than skating, not that he would say it aloud lest she get ideas that they should figure out a way to catapult her into the icy air.

"If you'll just hang on to us, I'm sure we can take a turn about the pond, nice and slow now."

Baldwyn looked heavenward then back to Benedict as if to say, "Do you think we have a chance of leaving her in the middle and feigning memory loss?"

"Faster," Agatha demanded.

"Aunt." Benedict cleared his throat. "If we go any faster, I believe you'll lose your breath and have one of those very real coughing fits." Very real his a—

"I said I would desire for you to take me faster, now do as I say."

Or reap the consequences, Benedict added mentally.

"As you wish." He increased his speed, as did Baldwyn and soon the dragon was smiling.

"This is my favorite part."

"Pardon?" Benedict nearly tripped. Was she just being polite?

"The wind, I miss the wind on my face. Makes an old woman feel alive." Her pale eyes looked at Benedict and a smile curved her lips. For such an ancient thing, she was quite beautiful still. His heart clenched as she turned her face upward and sighed.

Inwardly scolding himself for being so rude, Benedict tightened his grip on her arm. If she trusted them enough to close her eyes, if she was so completely within their clutches, he was going to do a blasted good job of keeping her standing straight, even if it killed him.

After a few minutes, Agatha sighed. "Stop! I'm cold, take me back to the house at once!" Agatha paused, and released their arms. "Baldwyn, Lady Anastasia looks quite frozen over on the bench, please see to her needs."

Benedict opened his mouth to speak, but Agatha interrupted, "And Benedict, do be sure that Lady Katherine is brought back to the house soon. She so desired to read this afternoon, and I would hate to see her too frozen to do so."

With that, Agatha, frail little Agatha skated off, at top speed, alone.

The little witch.

She knew exactly how to skate.

Why the devil did she…?

Separation. Benedict tossed his head back and laughed, torn between the desire to applaud her genius or strangle her for misinterpreting everything going on that afternoon, for she should know him well enough to know. His attraction was to Katherine, not Lady Anastasia.

He skated to Katherine and held out his hand. "Oh, no you don't," she teased. "Last time we skated, we both fell and you were peeking beneath my skirts."

"It isn't peeking if the skirt flies up."

"Says who?" Her eyes widened with indignation.

"I do."

"And let me guess, you're a duke so it has to count for something?"

"Look how well we are communicating, love." Benedict pulled her into a tight embrace, not caring that everyone around them was most likely staring. "So if I kiss you right now, it will not matter."

"B-because you're a duke."

"Precisely."

Katherine leaned in, her eyes half-closed.

"But," Benedict said when their foreheads touched, "I would hate to subject you to the whisperings and gossip, so another time then." He lifted her hand to his lips and kissed each knuckle before slipping her arm within his.

She tripped, nearly losing her footing.

"My, my, and to think I didn't even kiss your lips. I wonder if you would be able to walk in a straight line."

"Obviously I did before."

"But my kiss is different now," Benedict argued.

Katherine let out a loud sigh. "You're baiting me again. You want me to say, 'but how, Benedict? How is it different?' Then you'll lean in and wax poetic about how you'd love to show me Then I'd be breathless, you'd still be the Devil and I'd kick you in the shin. Sound about right?"

"Sometimes you frighten me." He shuddered.

"Perfect, so let us just skip ahead to the part after where you tell me all about why you felt the need to make Paisley jealous."

"Straight to the point, I like it." Benedict smirked. "At this rate, that of a snail or that of a disabled tortoise, Paisley will be happily engaged in holding her hand by the end of the year."

"I take it by your tone they need to be doing more than holding hands."

"Considering they will be married, yes that is the idea, nay the point, don't you think? One cannot beget an heir by osmosis."

"Osmosis?"

"The practice of—"

"I know what it means, I'm just curious as to why you used that particular analogy."

"We are on ice you know." Benedict quirked. "The examples are perfect. Besides, I have a plan."

"Of course you do."

Benedict grinned devilishly. His plan was more self-serving than he let Katherine believe. Could he help that he wanted her all to himself? So tonight, after dinner, he would make an absolute spectacle of himself, gaining her attention for the remainder of the evening. Hopefully after several bottles of port, his cousin would loosen up enough to attempt to converse with his *fiancée*. One could only hope that he wouldn't have to get the man foxed in order to do so.

Chapter Eighteen

The Christmas Carriage

Katherine left Benedict and went to her room to take a nap before dinner. However, the minute she closed her eyes, all she could see was his face. Foolish of her really, but it was impossible to concentrate on anything else.

Besides, he hadn't exactly told her his brilliant plan for the evening meal. She actually doubted he knew what he was going to do. His plan, it seemed, was to somehow separate the couples so Paisley was stuck with Lady Anastasia with no means to escape.

Sounded a lot like desperation, but if that's the only way to get them to pay attention to one another, then so be it. She still wasn't sure why she was helping, other than Benedict had asked it of her, and she soon found out that when the man smiled, when he leaned in and touched her arm just so, well she would most likely give him anything.

Which did not bode well for any future dark corners or hallways.

She did have some morals, though she felt them crumble every time she tasted his lips.

She shuddered and closed her eyes. Sleep, she just needed sleep.

****

Dinner started pleasantly. Benedict and Paisley sat across from one another at the head of the table, near Lord Marks, and Katherine and Lady Anastasia were across each man respectively.

After the first two courses, Katherine began to wonder if Benedict had lost his nerve.

And then, he leaned in toward Lady Anastasia and mumbled something that made her blush so brightly Katherine was ready to throw wine in the woman's face. Benedict pulled back, looking more pleased than he ought, then nodded to Katherine.

Clearing her throat, she leaned over and whispered nonsense about the weather into Paisley's ear, but at the last moment when his eyes turned to gaze into hers, she very gently placed a note in his hand.

He looked down, then up. She shook her head and reached for her wine.

The bait was set, now it was up to her to see if both parties would take it.

Once dinner was finished, Katherine kept a close eye on Paisley. He retired with the rest of the gentlemen, but as planned, within minutes he was walking down the hallway toward the far end of the study.

Perfect.

Katherine went in search of Benedict who was at that very moment walking down the same corridor with Lady Anastasia.

"You see, I cannot find the button, and it means the world to me!" Benedict pleaded with her. Though Katherine thought he was laying it on a little thick.

Most likely Lady Anastasia thought the only way to escape his presence was to actually go into the study and look for the blasted button.

"I'll just be here waiting, shouldn't follow you in, isn't proper and all that." Benedict coughed.

Katherine rolled her eyes from her hiding spot in the hall.

Once the door clicked shut, Katherine hurried to his side. "Tell me you have the key."

"Oh, I have the key. Did you know…" Benedict turned the lock. "That Lord Marks is quite the fellow. He offered to pay me to get those two together in such circumstances. Jolly fellow, should probably send him a Christmas ham."

Katherine stifled a laugh when she heard Paisley's voice begin to rise.

"How much port did he drink?" Katherine asked.

"Enough to hold her hand, possibly enough to be tempted to kiss her."

"What's wrong with you!" Katherine pinched him in the arm. "You had one job, well two. Get him foxed and find the key."

"Listen," Benedict pushed her against the wall playfully, his hands resting on her hips. "I did the best I could. What were you thinking wearing a dress like this?" He seemed mesmerized as his hands slowly caressed the satin.

"What?" Utterly confused and a bit tipsy from the many glasses of wine she drank at dinner, Katherine could do nothing but stare at him in disbelief. "What the devil does my dress have to do with anything?"

"Heavens, I love your dirty mouth." He winked, his hands still playing with the fabric, twisting the ribbon around her middle with his fingers. "Your dress, my lady, is distracting. You're lucky I was able to concentrate on the mission, let alone not drink myself into oblivion without touching you."

"Oh." She wished in that moment that she would have thought of a better response, but she was yet again dumbstruck by his dark sensual looks, his hooded eyes, and full lips.

"Shall we?" His voice was husky as he offered his arm.

Telling herself it was silly to shake or be nervous around someone she was marrying so soon, she nodded and gave him her arm.

Thinking he would lead her back to the party, she began to get somewhat alarmed when he escorted her outside.

"Where are we going?"

"It's a surprise," he mumbled in her hair before bestowing a kiss on her temple.

Far be it for her to argue a surprise.

Such a stark contrast between the glowing white snow and the dark sky. The moon hung in the sky like a picture. Benedict led her around to the front of the house, where a carriage was waiting.

"What's this?"

"Your Christmas surprise," he answered sweeping her into his arms and placing her in the seat. Fur blankets were stacked to the right, a bottle of wine and glasses in a basket to the left.

Grinning from ear to ear like a small child, Katherine managed not to throw her arms around his neck and laugh.

He remembered.

She had no idea he had listened that night when she was but seven years of age.

"I want my own Christmas carriage!" She wailed and wailed until her father announced he was going to sell all the carriages if she kept complaining.

"Silly goose." Benedict sat next to her. At fourteen, he seemed so much older, darker, and of course wiser.

"I'm not silly." Katherine crossed her arms and lifted her chin into the air, trying to prove to him that she was absolutely an adult who could make her own decisions, and at that point in her short life, she wanted her own Christmas carriage. "It just isn't fair." She sniffled and wiped her nose with her sleeve.

Benedict laughed then, a boy laugh that was more amused than mocking. "Then we shall just have to get you one, but not now, for your father looks ready to shoot anything that speaks."

Katherine giggled. "When, Ben? When can I have my own Christmas carriage?"

He pulled her to his side, she tucked her feet underneath her and sighed as the weight of his arm held her in a warm embrace. "How about I tell you a story, and in that story you'll see. Hmm?"

"Oh yes!" She clapped her hands with glee.

"One day when you are all grown up and going to lovely parties with sparkling ball gowns and handsome men..."

"Like you?" she asked, for she thought him quite handsome.

"Yes, like me." He blushed. "One of these days, you will catch the eye of one of those men, and he will proclaim his undying love to you. He'll offer to buy you any dress in the world if only you will love him. He'll offer to sail to the moon."

"That's silly!" Katherine covered her laughter with her hand. "One cannot sail to the moon!"

"Exactly my point, Kate, one cannot sail there, but his love will be so deep, that in his mind, he has already decided that if it is within your desires, he will find a way to do it."

Katherine sighed then, for she did not know that type of love existed.

Benedict had coughed and cleared his throat. "So, when that moment happens, when you see the stars shine in his eyes, when you see his eyes reflect the same feelings you have inside here," he tapped his own chest, "then you shall ask him for your Christmas carriage.

Because you waited, it will be even more special. You will also be sharing it with the person who cares the most for you in the world."

Katherine sighed. "I like that story. Is it true, Ben? Oh, tell me it is true!"

"I promise." *He ruffled her hair and kissed her on the cheek and she hopped up to bed, with dreams of Christmas carriages dancing in her head.*

Benedict's weight made the carriage tip, just slightly. "Do you like it?"

Katherine wasn't sure whether to laugh or cry. Instead she just stared at him, his face a mixture of apprehension and... love.

"Your eyes," she said.

"My eyes?"

"They reflect the stars." Katherine moved to sit near him, placing the blanket over both of their bodies. Benedict tapped the roof and they were off, in their Christmas carriage for a ride through the snow.

He kissed her, a feather-light kiss across the forehead. "Yes, love, yes they do."

Chapter Nineteen

Temptation, Thy Name is Katherine

Benedict wasn't sure if he was more amused, irritated, or pleased that Katherine had fallen asleep during their carriage ride.

He hadn't the heart to wake her up, not when her tiny hands reached inside his jacket and hugged his middle.

It was a shared moment, perhaps the most intimate moment of his life. To have a woman, in her sleep, completely trust him, forsaking her own safety and sanity, and cling to him. Well, it made him feel like the past few years of his life had been for nothing but selfishness. What had he been thinking?

He looked down at her sleeping form. This feeling, this raw desire, this primal need to protect her from everything even if it killed him, was what he had been missing. And he hated himself for being so blind and stupid.

In fact, he was quite ready to shout it to the world, but again, he didn't want to ruin the moment.

He could have spent hours watching her sleep. The way her lips fell slightly open, her eyelashes resting against her pale skin. Her furrowed brows when she must have been dreaming, and the way her breathing seemed to lull him into a relaxed state, he could listen to her breathe all day.

And again he was hit with that thought, he had completely and totally fallen for this bewitching beauty, his childhood nemesis, the one girl he thought he couldn't possibly come to care for in such a way, let alone bring himself to marry.

The carriage pulled to a halt. He carefully lifted Katherine into his arms and carried her quietly up the stairs and into her chambers.

The desire to stay with her was such a strong pull. He was half-tempted to run naked in the snow in order to shake him from his feelings.

His valet would love that.

At least he'd been wearing clothes as of late, and at least trying to be amiable to the man. It wasn't his fault he didn't like being fussed over or touched by a man in places no man should be touched by another man.

Regardless, he managed to set her on her bed, and kiss her just lightly across the lips before walking to the door.

"Benedict?" Her voice was groggy from sleep.

"Yes?" *Run, run!* His head screamed at him, old habits died hard, and he wanted desperately to show her how much he cared for her, to make her his before the vows were said.

"Thank you for my Christmas carriage."

His heart melted, then began hammering in his chest, it was nearly painful, the way her words affected him, making him want to hit himself in order to return to reality.

"You're welcome." His hand touched the door.

"Benedict?"

"Yes," he near growled. She had no idea the danger she

was in of losing that precious virginity a week before she planned.

"Stay."

Fighting the urge to roar like a Neanderthal, Benedict chuckled. "Love, that wouldn't be a good idea."

"Please?" She rose from the bed just slightly, her hair falling across her shoulders in waves. His imagination would never be able to dream up a woman of her beauty, of the absolute devastating pull she had on him.

"If I stay..." Benedict groaned and leaned his head against the door. "I'll only stay until you're once again asleep, love, then I need to leave."

She sighed and lay back down on the bed.

He walked cautiously to the other side, not bothering to take off his boots, for that would be the beginning of the end. As far as his body was concerned, taking his boots off while lying next to a beautiful woman meant he was about to take off the rest of his clothes.

And he wasn't sure he would be able to stop with his boots.

Hilarious that the Devil Duke would need to keep his boots on in order to keep his lust in check.

"Sleep." He kissed her forehead, but she reached up and pulled his head closer to hers, opening her mouth to him.

He should have run.

He should have escaped when he had the chance.

He should have said no.

Hang honor, hang it all.

His lips crushed hers, Benedict's hands grasped her wrists pinning her to the bed as he nipped her lower lip, tugging it between his teeth.

She moaned.

He cursed then straddled her because at the time it seemed the only option, not that it was intelligent by any stretch of the imagination.

Her body fit perfectly underneath him. Of course it would. He tugged at her bodice, pulling it down to her waist.

And then froze.

Time stood still.

He hated he was using such clichés in his mind, yet time did seem to stand still as he glimpsed her.

Bewildered that he was able to think beyond pleasuring her, he slowly pulled her bodice back up and kissed her gently across her lips.

"I'm going to give you more."

"What?" Her eyelashes fluttered against her cheeks. "You don't want to…"

"I want to give you the moon." He kissed her cheek. "I want to give, not take."

She nodded.

"Kate, you are far too special, and I fear it would be over before it began, for I find I'm having trouble controlling myself at this moment."

She smiled and touched his face with her hand.

"Goodnight, my sweet."

"Goodnight," she mumbled then turned to her side and closed her eyes.

****

To say that Benedict had a good night's sleep would have been a grotesque lie straight from the pit of Hades.

He did not, in fact, have a good night, nor did he sleep.

Oh, he was prone to exaggeration, this much was true, but when his valet came into the room to help him dress, he was already sitting in front of the fire, twiddling his thumbs, or if he was being completely honest with himself, thinking of Katherine.

"Your grace?" His valet's eyes were so incredibly wide it was amusing, except for the fact that Benedict was grumpy and tired, and truth be told, slightly aroused, even still. God save him.

"Well, let's get on with it," Benedict snapped. When he looked in the mirror he nearly burst out laughing, apparently insanity was a close friend whilst running on little to no sleep. But he couldn't help himself.

"You're drunk then?" It was a statement from his otherwise stiff-necked valet. No doubt he was used to seeing Benedict at his worst.

But that's what kept making him laugh. He had stayed up all night, thinking about one woman. He wasn't out with his mistresses, nor was he at the gambling hells. He was simply sitting in a chair, and he looked like he had just spent the night in the worst parts of London.

"No," he answered. "I'm not drunk, but I will admit to being slightly unstable, in the emotional sort of way, so if you'll be quick about your duties. I have a woman to attend to."

"Always do."

"What was that?" Benedict snapped.

"Good for you." His valet smiled cheekily and patted his back smoothing out the lines of the coat. "It is the best I can do in your drunken state, your grace."

"Again, I'm not drunk."

"If you say so."

Benedict pointed to the door. His valet lifted up his hands in mock fear and walked out. That was the problem having the best valet money could buy—he could afford to have an attitude.

Benedict clapped his hands together and nearly ran out the door, tumbling right into a woman.

"Apologies, I…"

Katherine looked up with bright eyes and a shy smile. "Benedict." Her chest heaved though he knew it couldn't possibly be exertion.

"How did you sleep?" she asked.

"Like a baby," he lied and offered his arm. "So, what shall we do today?"

"Well," Katherine blushed just slightly, the color bringing a rosy hue to her delicate cheekbones. "I thought perhaps we could have a snowball fight."

"In public?" He placed a hand over his chest and pretended to be offended. "My dear, dukes do not run around in public throwing snowballs. I don't know what anyone has told you about me but…"

She threw back her head and laughed. "But, good sir, I was under the impression that dukes can do anything!"

"If only." Lust pounded in his veins, he clenched his fists as he watched her eyes dilate and lips part. "Perhaps we better join the others."

"Perhaps." The minx winked and reached for his arm.

****

One fort, three snowball fights, all of which she lost, and two meals later, and Katherine was utterly exhausted. It took everything within her not to take a nap before dinner.

Once dinner was finished, she could barely keep her eyes open. But she didn't want to miss a thing. Benedict had been called back to Town that evening on business, so he was ordering servants around in order to rush back in time. Though he needn't meet with his solicitor until morning, he apparently wanted to get a head start, which was a tad frustrating for Katherine, but she didn't mind. She'd follow a few hours later and would soon be in London, waiting to marry the man she used to despise.

Lord Marks cleared his throat. "I thought a few games of whist would revive some of you after this day's festivities. You will find several tables set up in the purple salon as well as sherry and port. Please, enjoy your final night here."

A loud thumping was heard, but it couldn't have been Agatha, ever since the ice-skating she had taken to her room feigning illness, or in Benedict's words, just biding her time until she snapped at one of them again.

The thumping continued, until finally Katherine turned around. Lord Marks was hitting his cane on the corner of his boot.

The rest of the dinner party had left, leaving them alone.

"May I ask a favor of you, Lady Katherine?"

"Of course."

He leaned forward. "I appreciate what his grace and you have done in respect to the Duke of Paisley and my daughter. I was wondering if you won't give me one more boon before everyone leaves?"

"Absolutely."

"My daughter, she is very competitive. Why don't we arrange for you and Baldwyn to sit near one another, perhaps be partners in a few games. I think it might be the very thing to get her to admit her feelings. I believe as a father I'm resorting to jealousy to get my daughter to become vulnerable. I hope I do not live to regret it."

Katherine smiled. "You won't, and I'll do my best."

Which she did.

Three hours later, she and Paisley were laughing so hard she nearly fell out of her chair, and it was all because he could not play the game to save his life. He was awful. Terrible more like it.

Lady Anastasia was never without wine in her hand, and after a while Katherine became a little more than nervous that Lady Anastasia was going to topple over. Instead, her face became redder by the minute until finally she had an outburst.

"The two of you are rather cozy. And where is the Duke of Banbury at present, Lady Katherine?" Lady Anastasia coolly eyed Paisley as well as Katherine, a bitter smile spreading across her lips.

Unfortunately everyone was privy to her little speech.

Causing the game to stop.

And Paisley to grow pale.

"You know well, Lady Anastasia, that my *fiancé* has retired early." Katherine kept her gaze level on Anastasia, hoping to convey the message for her to stop making a scene in front of everyone and embarrassing poor Paisley, for it was evident that he cared for her so. But the women continued to talk.

"How fortunate for Paisley."

Katherine gasped, then quickly offered her apologies and went in search of Benedict, for she hadn't meant to hurt Lady Anastasia's feelings, at least not in that way. She had only hoped to spur the girl on as Lord Marks had suggested. The wine did not prove helpful, that much was sure.

She ran up the stairs to Benedict's chambers, nearly out of breath when she knocked on his door.

Chapter Twenty

A Man's Shame

Knock, Knock, Knock.

Benedict went to the door to open it, but the person on the other side was obviously in a losing battle with patience, it swung wide nearly hitting him in the face.

"Should have known," he grumbled.

"Sorry," Katherine said. "May we leave now?"

"In the evening?" Benedict scowled. "I meant to leave first thing in the morning. Do you think you can practice patience until then?"

She bit her lip and crossed her arms.

"What happened?"

"Hmm?" She gave him an innocent look, much like a cat hiding a mouse under its paw.

"What happened?" he repeated, grasping her crossed arms and pulling her closer into his embrace.

"Lady Anastasia drank too much, yelled at me, made me feel a fool, and now I just want to go home."

Was she crying?

"See? That wasn't too hard." He lifted her quivering chin and kissed a fallen tear. "We'll leave immediately."

Within a half hour, they were in the carriage on their way back into London.

"Now." Benedict patted Katherine's hand. "Tell me what is really going on in that little head."

Katherine smiled. "Well, you see. I think Anastasia loves your cousin desperately, and she accused me of flirting with him, which is ridiculous. He was my partner in cards, nothing more."

Benedict fought the surge of jealousy.

"It doesn't matter. She yelled and was quite embarrassed and left the room. Paisley went after her, and I just figured it would be better if we were not at the house. That way, he cannot go looking for you when he gets afraid of the woman, and she cannot spend time apologizing to me." She proceeded to tell him about her and Lord Marks' agreement.

"My dear, are you matchmaking?"

She looked at her hands.

"You and Agatha truly should not live in the same city, you do know that?"

"I love her."

"Who?"

Katherine sighed. "Agatha. I think she's brilliant."

"Yes, but you also trip over your own feet and show your knees in public."

"Very funny." Katherine made a face and raised her voice. "But truthfully, she's lovely!"

"Keep your voice down. She'll hear you!" Benedict all but shouted.

"In the carriage? But she's at the house. She's been sleeping for an entire day!"

"She has her ways." Benedict outwardly shuddered.

"Now, let us have some rest before I deliver you to your home."

Seconds after saying those very words the carriage jerked to a halt. Benedict peered through the window looking for the reason, and then a rap was heard at the door.

He opened it. "Problem?"

"Your grace, a wheel is stuck. It seems the snow is too deep, and we need to go back, but it's at least a two mile walk back up the drive, and in this weather…" The footman shuddered. "I think it best that you and the lady stay here in the safety of the carriage."

Benedict wasn't sure exactly how safe she would be in the carriage with him, but he didn't say it aloud. Instead he thought quite hard about their situation, waiting in the carriage meant they would still be freezing by the time his footman made it back. Even if they did take the horses.

His eyes scanned the road ahead of him, then back toward the house.

"There." He pointed. "What's that?"

"The hunting cabin?" the footman asked. "It's for tenants and those who like to hunt on the countryside. I dare say there may be some wood to build a fire."

"Right." Benedict hopped out of the carriage and held out his hand to Katherine. "We're to go on a little jaunt."

"A jaunt?" she repeated, teeth chattering.

"Yes, or adventure. Would you rather I use the word adventure? How about if I say it's a Christmas adventure, hmm?"

Katherine's eyes narrowed.

"No? Alright." He placed her arm within his and trudged with her through the snow. "I thought rather than freezing to death in that carriage, that we would build a fire in that lovely looking cabin over yonder."

"That?" she repeated, dread filling her voice. "It looks

haunted."

"It's nothing of the sort," he assured her. "It's merely dark, besides things aren't allowed to be haunted during the holiday season."

"Says who?"

"I say, and I'm a duke, so the ghosts have to listen."

"Arrogance, arrogance." She laughed, but followed him to the cabin, within minutes they were inside. He helped Katherine to a chair and searched for wood.

Fortunately, the moonlight mixed with the set of matches he had acquired the night before, while smoking cheroots with the gentlemen, helped shed enough light that he was able to locate where the wood was hiding.

Soon, he had a roaring fire, and was thankful to feel heat begin to radiate from the hearth.

He motioned for Katherine to sit near him by the fireplace.

It was a tiny hunting lodge, nothing to boast about truly. It held one small bed in the corner, a table in the middle of the room, and two sitting chairs in front of the fire. No stove to speak of and no food.

Pity, for his stomach needed sustenance.

As if on cue, it growled.

Katherine smirked. "Hungry?"

"Only for you," he teased, though the sudden plummet in his stomach should have hinted him toward the truth of those very words.

They were alone, very alone.

He should have laughed at their circumstances, was he not merely days ago planning on fully ruining the girl in hopes that she would cry off? And the day after finally giving up and realizing how deeply he cared for her, he found himself completely alone with the girl.

His conscience fought an epic inner battle as his eyes

continued to rake over her with a mixture of desire and interest.

"When will we marry?" Katherine asked, breaking the silence.

Benedict wasn't sure what the correct answer was to be. After all, weddings were sort of a sacred ritual to women. They were cause for great joy, weeping, insanity...so he needed to tread carefully. "When would you like to marry?"

"Oh, you mean it?" She clasped her hands together in excitement allowing him to exhale with relief.

"Of course." His chest puffed, just slightly.

"Tomorrow, let's marry tomorrow."

"Pardon?" He coughed.

"Tomorrow," she said slower and reached out to touch his arm. "I'm already ruined. We both know I don't need any sort of fanfare. After all, the *ton* has seen my knees, have they not?"

Benedict chuckled.

"I know we wanted to wait until after the Kringle Ball, but I truly cannot wait to start our lives. Don't you agree?"

He suddenly felt very, very hot, and deuced uncomfortable, and the innocent look in her eyes haunted him.

"Er, yes." He rubbed the back of his neck.

"To think! In just a few hours, I'll be able to move into your house, and we'll be able to..." She blushed profusely and looked at her hands.

"Be able to?" He leaned forward and lifted one eyebrow in question.

"You know..."

"No, I truly don't."

Her look was incredulous. "Benedict!"

"Katherine."

She scowled. "We'll be able to really be together."

"Like we are now?" He played innocent. Gads how he loved the way she became so easily flustered. Her cheeks took on the most beautiful shade of pink, tempting his tongue to caress the spot right below her jaw where the pink met ivory skin.

"No, not like we are now." Her little bum shifted in the chair.

He leaned even closer, placing both hands on either side of the chair until his face was so near, he could hear her shallow breaths. "You mean like this?" His hands reached out to touch her neck and then moved down her shoulders, her arms, and finally to her legs. With little effort, he lifted her into his arms showing her how to wrap herself around him, and just held her there as he placed long lingering kisses on her neck and face.

"Y-yes…Oh, heavens yes, like this." Her head fell back exposing her throat.

Careful, his inner voice warned him. *Take it slow.*

But he was never one to listen to his good conscience.

So he laid her across the dusty bed and hovered over her, watching her squirm and sigh beneath his touch.

"Benedict." Her voice was hoarse.

"Yes, love?"

"Will your servants like me?"

What an odd question. And dreadful timing considering his hand was already placed halfway up her creamy thigh.

He kept his arousal in check and tried to answer the question, mentally going through every person in his employ.

And then his body went cold.

Maria.

Suddenly, he was disgusted with himself. Withdrawing his hand from the pleasure of her leg, he leaned back on the bed and shuddered.

"What is it?" Katherine asked.

"It's just that…" Benedict couldn't even look her in the eyes his shame was so great. "I had forgotten about some business at the house, business I need to attend to before I welcome you with open arms."

"Oh." She looked down.

"But..." he interjected. "It won't take long. Before you know it, you'll be the mistress of the house." He gulped against the bile that rose in his throat at the use of the word mistress. Could he have not come up with a better description? She was so much better than that.

And he, the Devil, did not deserve her.

If she knew...

Well, if she knew, she wouldn't continue to give him a chance. He was afraid, devil take it, he was terrified that if she truly knew about some of the things that took place under the roof of that house, she would be more than scandalized.

"Let me buy you a house." The words fell out of his mouth in a rush.

"A house? You want to buy me a house?" Katherine shook her head. "Whatever's wrong with your house?"

"It's old."

"All right..." Katherine's eyes searched his. "And you want to buy a newer house, is that it?"

"Yes. I want you to have the best." At least that part was true.

"I'll buy you a house, move you into it..." Why in the blazes was he going on in this fashion? As if she was some type of mistress. "Naturally, I'll live there too," he added.

"I should hope so." Katherine laughed. "We are to be married." She lifted her hand to cup his face. "After all, you won't get a traditional *ton* marriage from me."

"I won't?" He feigned depression, though he couldn't have been more pleased.

"No." The minx leaned closer to him, her arm hooking his neck like a shepherd's crook, pulling him down closer and closer until he once again hovered over her. "I'll want you by my side every day."

"That can be arranged."

"And in my bed every night."

What was that? Angels singing?

"I believe I can manage to agree to your terms."

"Promise." Her eyes sparkled in the moonlight.

He took a shuddering breath before lowering his lips to hers and mumbling against them, "Promise."

Now all he needed to do was make sure she never found out his secret, never know the depths of his depravity, lest she lose that sparkle he so adored.

****

Something was bothering Benedict, though Katherine hadn't a clue what it could be. By all standards, he was acting the perfect gentleman.

That should have been her first hint.

Originally she had thought he was going to seduce her, not that she minded one whit.

And then he had pulled back, a look of absolute horror on his face as he began to sputter nonsense about buying a new house.

He was wealthy. Everyone knew how wealthy, even though he gambled as if he truly desired to lose his entire fortune. He never lost.

So it could not be lack of funds.

She bit her lip and looked at him again. Benedict had kissed her and then told her to sleep.

As if she could sleep after his hands had been halfway up her thigh.

Ridiculous!

Perhaps, she thought as she closed her eyes and tried to relax, he was embarrassed about the state of his house? After all, bachelors were known to be careless in their décor as well as their upkeep. The poor man probably didn't even pay a full staff.

What his house needed was a woman's touch! There was no need for him to spend money for her sake.

A smile curved her lips. That was it! She would surprise him. Tomorrow after he dropped her off, she would quickly change, and then arrive at his house and offer her help. After all, the way things were going, they were planning on gaining a special license as soon as possible. It wasn't as if she was not ruined already.

With a grin, she finally relaxed enough to try to sleep, all the while thinking of ways she could surprise Benedict.

Chapter Twenty-one

Not All Surprises Are Welcome

By the time the carriage dropped off Katherine at her home, it was some ungodly time of the night. At least two or three a.m.

The footman had taken another hour to trudge back to the cabin with different transportation. The snow storm had let up enough for them to continue on.

Though there was a part of Benedict that wished he and Katherine could have stayed in that cabin forever, away from his past, away from his uncertain future.

Stupidity seemed to be the only way to describe his actions. How had he not remembered Maria?

Or the six before her?

Exhausted, his legs felt as if he had poured sand into his boots. Slowly, he made his way into his house, not bothering to deal with the situation as of yet. He would need energy and sustenance to do what he had to do.

He pushed open the door to his room and cursed.

"I've been waiting for you," a lush feminine voice said in the darkness.

He wanted to hit something. How the devil did she know he would be arriving at such a time?

"You must be exhausted," the throaty voice continued. "Let me relieve some of that tension, your grace."

"No." His response was cold, angry.

"No?" Maria laughed as Benedict lit the candle nearest the bed.

The woman was draped with nothing but a sheet, her hair tumbling around her waist, a coquettish pout on her lips. "Feisty tonight, hmm?"

Benedict pinched his nose and prayed for patience. "Listen to me."

She leaned forward giving him a view that made him ill with disgust.

"If you do not leave within the next five seconds, I'm going to remove you myself, and I guarantee you there will be nothing sensual or erotic about it. Now, get out of my bed chambers."

Maria's smile fell, her eyes narrowed. "Is this a new game?"

"No!" he yelled. "Get out!"

Slowly, because Maria was provocative about everything, she pulled back the blankets of the bed, exposing herself to him. With languid movements, she reached for the nearest robe, wrapped it around her naked body and with a seething glare, slammed the door.

"That went well." Benedict cursed again, then tumbled into bed. It was too late, and he was too irritated and upset with himself to deal with the woman tonight. In the morning…he would fix everything in the morning.

And hire a new housekeeper as soon as possible.

His eighth in the past two years.

Meaning, he had been going through at least four mistresses a year, hiring each of them as his housekeeper in order to keep things…

Convenient.

Their jobs were simple: be available to pleasure him at all hours of the day and night, and he would not only pay them a salary, but on their parting terms give them a special bonus.

He laughed bitterly.

A bonus?

For what?

Sex?

Convenience?

Utterly sickened, he closed his eyes and tried to sleep. Tomorrow would be the day the Devil came to terms with his demons.

****

Katherine woke earlier than usual and quickly dressed in a simple white muslin. If she was to be decorating and surprising Benedict, she didn't need to wear anything more lavish.

Besides, she would not be making any morning or afternoon calls. At least not today.

Excited for her idea, she quickly went to Bond Street and made several appointments for the house redecorating. Giddy with excitement, she made her way to Benedict's house.

It was located in Mayfair, much like hers. But it was big, so much bigger than she imagined it would be.

Nervous, she bit her lip and knocked.

A crisp-looking butler opened the door and peered down at her through spectacles.

"His grace has enough servants."

Katherine laughed. Did she truly look that horrendous?

"No, I'm sure his grace wouldn't mind for me to visit. You see, I'm his *fiancée*."

At that, the butler's lips quirked into a smile and then his eyes darkened. "You poor thing."

"Pardon?"

He sighed. "I'll see if he is receiving callers. Why don't I show you to the Lavender room? Would you care for some tea, miss?"

"Lady Katherine Bourne." She curtsied and immensely enjoyed the blush that crept up the butler's neck.

"Pardon, did you say Lady Katherine Bourne?"

"Yes."

"W-well, why don't you have a seat, there, right there." His shaky hand pointed to the settee. "And I'll have Ma—" he coughed. "That is to say, I will have someone, anyone bring you tea."

"Alright." She smiled warmly and leaned back against the sofa, taking in the beautiful room surrounding her.

It was in purples and eggshell colors, beautiful actually, not masculine at all. After a few minutes, she began to feel the need to snoop. After all, he was to be her husband in a manner of days.

Her eyes fell on the large bookcase on the far end of the room. Her gloved hand traced the furniture as she made her way to the books and began reading the titles.

Odd, they were all in strange languages. Curious, she picked one up.

And promptly dropped it to the floor.

What type of man kept books with pictures like, like that?

She tried another.

Same thing.

And another, until she had looked through at least ten books. All of them with graphic pictures she would never be able to remove from her memory as long as she lived.

Carefully, she put them all back, the last one, however had fallen on its spine causing the first page to flutter open.

My love, Maria.

Who in the blazes was Maria?

A sudden commotion took place outside the doors. A woman's voice. A man's, and then suddenly the door burst open.

A beautiful woman with dark hair and dark eyes came into the room. Her uniform was typical of a servant, and in her hand was a tray with tea and biscuits.

"Hello," Katherine greeted.

The woman glared.

Katherine cleared her throat. "You must be the housekeeper?" she guessed.

"Yes," the woman answered crisply.

A butler who stuttered and laughed, and a beautiful exotic woman with the manners of a streetwalker.

Apparently before any decoration was to take place, Benedict needed a new staff.

"Please, sit." The woman's eyes fell to the book in Katherine's hands then snapped back up to her face. "Find anything interesting, my lady?"

"O-oh, this? No, no, it fell, so I was putting it back." She felt heat rise to her cheeks as she pushed the book into its rightful place and shuffled back to the sofa where the woman was laying out the biscuits and tea.

Katherine couldn't help but notice how striking the woman was. She could not be much older than Katherine herself. Jealousy surged, but Katherine fought it with everything in her. Perhaps Benedict was extending a courtesy. After all, a woman this striking would surely find herself in a house of ill repute if left to her own devices to survive. Shame washed over her jealousy.

As the woman made a curtsy to leave, Katherine reached

out the only way she knew how, politeness. "Thank you... Apologies, I did not catch your name?" Not that it was typical for ladies to ask such things, but this woman did not need to know that.

The woman gave a hollow laugh. "Maria, his grace's seventh housekeeper in two years."

Odd. "Does he have trouble keeping housekeepers, Maria?" Katherine asked with amusement tickling her voice.

Maria turned cold eyes to Katherine. "Let us just say his grace has a variety of tastes."

****

Benedict awoke with a start.

His butler, Marsail, hovered over him, worry etched in his every feature.

"What the devil are you doing in my room?"

Marsail cleared his throat. "A young lady is here to see you, your grace. I thought it best to keep her away from other parts of the house, but I fear..."

"Who? Who is it?" Benedict demanded.

Marsail began to perspire. "She claims she is your *fiancée*, but that is a ridiculous notion, is it not?" He patted his forehead with a handkerchief.

Benedict reached for Marsail's coat and pulled him close. "Tell me that Maria is no longer here. Tell me that Lady Katherine has been locked in the very room you put her in."

Marsail looked away. "Maria stole the key."

"How does a tiny woman steal a key from you, of all people?"

Marsail began to shake.

"Never mind." Benedict cursed and pulled on his clothes in rapid fashion. His valet rolled his eyes when he strolled into the room, but aided in making him presentable, mumbling something under his breath that at least his grace was choosing to wear clothes after such a late evening.

Benedict chose not to comment.

He raced down the stairs and pushed open the doors to the Lavender room with such urgency he could have sworn they were going to fly off their hinges.

Katherine sat prim and proper, tea in hand, but her eyes were distant.

"Katherine?"

She licked her lips. "I shouldn't have come." She placed her tea on the table and rose.

"No, don't." Benedict reached out to her, but she pulled away.

"Benedict."

"Yes?" His voice felt shaky. Devil take it, he was nearly trembling with fear, shame…all of the above.

"Why have you had seven housekeepers in the last two years? Why would a man need that many replacements… unless…"

She was assuming the worst, not that he didn't deserve it. "You should sit back down."

"I don't want to sit back down!" she yelled, her arms clenched at her sides. "Explain to me why you would need so many housekeepers." Her eyes pleaded with his. It was as if she was begging him to lie, to tell her that her suspicions were not correct.

He looked down at the floor. He couldn't bear to look at her, not now.

She walked toward him then. He saw her shoes beneath her dress, and slowly raised his eyes to meet her face.

"Tell me," she said.

"A man doesn't need seven housekeepers in two years, not unless he's the absolute devil. Not unless he hires them to be his live-in mistress. Not unless he's so deranged that he values convenience above all else."

"Alright." Katherine bit her lip. "Alright." She repeated, her head nodding up and down as if she was trying to make sense of the information.

"But..." Benedict grabbed her arms and pulled her against him. "I'm not that man anymore. I cannot be that man."

Katherine said nothing.

"I-I..." Benedict cursed. "I promise you, I had every intention of getting rid of Maria last night when—"

"When?" Katherine's eyes narrowed.

"When I was in his bed," Maria's voice announced from the entryway. "Isn't that right, Benedict?"

Katherine jerked back in horror.

"You are a witch." Benedict glared at Maria. "Leave my house this instant."

"But what about your promise?" Maria tilted her head.

Benedict groaned.

"Promise?" Katherine asked.

"Yes, you see, his grace here is so brilliant in the way he hires mistresses. We live and work here, and then when he cuts us loose, as he's doing this moment, he settles us a grand sum of money for our troubles. I take it," Maria looked Katherine up and down, "That you will be housekeeper number eight?"

"That's it!" Katherine yelled and surged forward. Benedict didn't stop her, mainly because he knew he deserved whatever physical blow she would deal him.

But it wasn't him she was charging after.

Nor was it him that she hit, repeatedly.

He really shouldn't be amused. It wasn't the time to laugh, but seeing Katherine claw at Maria was a proud moment for him.

Maria screamed until finally Katherine relented and

pushed her. "If you ever speak of me in that way again, I'll kill you."

Benedict wanted to add how truthful she was being. After all she had nearly killed him, how many times on accident now?

Katherine continued to push Maria until she was out of the room. "And if I ever see you here again, I'll not hesitate to shoot you. His grace will stay true to his promise. He will give you the money you deserved, spreading your legs like a whore. But know, this man," she pointed back to Benedict with fire in her eyes, "is mine. Do I make myself clear?"

Maria nodded several times before gathering her skirts and running out the front door.

Katherine's whole body shook.

Benedict couldn't comfort her, couldn't touch her, not after everything. Never had he felt so dirty, so debased. To see his innocent *fiancée* yell at his former mistress after revealing so much about his affairs. He could not bear it. Could not fathom it.

He truly was the Devil Duke.

"Benedict," Katherine said without turning. "You will still marry me."

It wasn't a question.

"If you'll have me."

"One question." Her hands opened and closed at her sides as if she was trying to regain feeling in her fingers.

"Yes."

"Last night, did you—"

"No!" he yelled, and then, "Absolutely not! You must know how I feel about you, Katherine. I would not do that to you. I have not touched another woman since that first night at the ball."

"Good," she said tersely.

"Good?" He shuffled closer to her.

"Yes." She whipped around and charged toward him.

Here it comes.

"You are mine. Mine, you devil! If I ever catch you with another woman, if you as much as grin at a woman in the next ten years of our marriage, I'll castrate you. Do I make myself clear?"

"Crystal." Heaven help him, he loved her. He wanted to tell her, to fall to his knees. It wasn't the time. Would it ever be the time?

"Fine." She pushed away from him and walked to the door.

"Katherine," he called.

She stopped.

"I'm sorry. I'm so sorry." The words seemed too shallow, not deep enough to convey how wretched he felt, how he wanted to cut himself open and bleed all over the floor.

Benedict wasn't sure how long he stood there immobile. Matters became worse when people continued to shuffle in throughout the day in hopes to help redecorate a few rooms as a surprise-wedding gift from Katherine.

He was a cad.

He wasn't sure if he should get foxed.

Shoot himself in the foot.

Or just apologize again and again until she knew he meant it.

He started with flowers. As many as he could order, and sent them to her house. No response.

So he became creative.

He bought her a horse. Stupid idea really, what the devil was she going to do with an extra horse?

And then a thought occurred to him. When they were young, she had always liked to read. Books were her favorite pasttime, the little bluestocking.

With a smile, he placed his next order.

Books, lots and lots of books.

When his final gift elicited no response, he decided to make his way over there in person.

"Lady Katherine is indisposed and not receiving callers, your grace." The butler's expression was heated. Benedict half-expected his coattails to catch on fire.

"Do you know if she at least received the books?" Benedict asked.

At that, the butler's face broke into an amused smile. "Ah yes, I believe the lady mentioned something about using the books for kindling in place of wood. Brilliant idea, if I say so myself. Good day." The butler shut the door.

In his face. A duke's face nonetheless.

Benedict cursed and looked up at the large house, scaling the wall was out of the question.

Desperate, he ran around to the back.

Spying. He was now resorting to spying on the woman he was to marry.

A door opened, Katherine emerged onto the balcony, a sad smile on her lips. "Is he gone?"

"Yes, my lady." The maid curtsied. "Will that be all?"

"Yes, but, next time he arrives, allow him into the sitting room. I shall see him now."

Benedict almost ran back to the front of the house to knock on the door, but something in Katherine's expression gave him pause.

And then he saw them. Watery tears running down her cheeks. She lifted her dainty hand to wipe them away then let out a guttural sigh before laying her head against the rail of the balcony and hiding her face in her hands.

He was the reason.

Suddenly, he felt quite at odds with himself. As if he had put his boots on the wrong feet. Having made a mess of things, he knew the only person he could trust to give him adequate advice was the one person he never expected to be seeking wisdom from.

Agatha.

She should be arriving today.

After all, she was to make an appearance at the Kringle Ball in a few days, and she would want to rest up before she did so.

A new plan began to form in his head, one that caused a slight smile to replace the frown.

Chapter Twenty-two

A Sad End, A New Beginning

Benedict appointed his very best footman to stand watch by his aunt's house. The minute she arrived, he wanted to know.

Hours later, he was knocking on the door with such force, he thought it would come off the hinges.

"Yes?" Baldwyn answered, odd. Where the devil was the butler? The minute his eyes fell on Benedict, he exhaled and pulled him into a hug. "I saw you from the window, by the time Agatha's old butler would have made it here, you would have been an old man."

Coughing was heard from behind Baldwyn. He rolled his eyes.

Benedict stepped into the house; it felt odd, almost eerie. "What's going on? Something's wrong." But everything seemed to be in place. From the perfectly calm servants to the sparkling floors.

Everything but…Agatha.

Dread shot down his spine, Benedict looked at Baldwyn with a questioning gaze. "I take it she's resting."

Baldwyn lifted his arm and scratched the back of his head, and it was then that Benedict was able to focus on his cousin's horrendous demeanor.

"What the devil happened to you?"

"Life," Baldwyn muttered. "Agatha, Anastasia, marriage, and a half-empty bottle of brandy, thanks for asking."

Benedict squinted and leaned in toward his cousin. "Let's start with the first one, though I can't help you with life, considering I've mucked up my own and that of the woman I love quite thoroughly. Let's discuss Agatha."

At the mention of her name, a nearby maid burst into tears and ran from the entryway.

Was the woman that much of a dragon to her own staff?

"She's not well." Baldwyn swallowed and looked away, his eyes glassy from being foxed or perhaps depressed.

"I need to speak with her."

"Follow me." Baldwyn led him to Agatha's chambers. "I'll just be outside while you two have a little chat."

Benedict opened the door and paused. "Baldwyn?"

"Hmm?"

"Do you love her?"

Baldwyn paled. "Agatha? Of course, you fool, anyone would—"

"Not Agatha. Anastasia. Do you love her?"

Immediately Baldwyn looked to the ground. "Yes."

"Then you should tell her before you lose her forever."

Benedict slapped his cousin on the shoulder and walked into the large room. It reeked of medicine and tonics. Confused, he looked from left to right until his eyes finally settled on a lump in the bed.

"Aunt?" He walked closer, irritated at the ridiculous knot of emotion in his throat.

"Benedict? Is that you?" Her voice was raspy and weak.

"Yes." He sat on the bed and grasped her frail hand. "Are you feeling under the weather?"

"Oh, it will blow over, it always does." Agatha waved him off with her other hand. "So, what brings you here? I can only imagine the amount of pride you swallowed to seek me out. Surprised you made it up the stairs without cursing me to perdition."

Benedict chuckled, his hand slowly caressing hers. "It seems I've some more pride to swallow, if you'll allow me."

"Always." Her eyes twinkled, but her face was still far too pale for his liking.

"Well, I don't really know how to start."

"Remember, I do love your stories. Let us start at the beginning, shall we?" With a sigh, she tried to squeeze his hand though it was a vain effort for the thing had little strength in her.

"Katherine, she won't, that is to say she won't…"

"Marry you?" Agatha interrupted.

"No, she'll still marry me."

"Then she's disagreeable?"

"No, she's amiable, perfect really." *The most beautiful woman I've ever seen*, he wanted to add.

"Did she offend you in some way then?" Agatha coughed and reached for the water. He helped her take a sip and shook his head.

"No, I'm afraid it is I who has done the offending, though I wasn't aware that my past actions would overshadow my future happiness, it seems I've done just that. I've ruined it."

Agatha tilted her head. "But you say she's still going to marry you?"

"Yes."

"Then what is the problem?" Agatha's eyebrows furrowed.

"She won't forgive me."

"But she'll marry you?" Agatha repeated. She truly must be sick for she never wasted time repeating anything, if he wasn't fortunate enough to hear her the first time, well the loss was his, and he would undoubtedly suffer for it.

"Yes," he said slowly.

A smile broke out across her weathered face. "So you wish for something more than marriage. Is this what I'm understanding?"

"Well, I…" Benedict paused, thinking quite seriously on his aunt's simple words. "I want more, but I also want to give her more. I want…" He looked away, a lump forming in his throat. Devil take it, he could not cry over a girl.

"Everything." Agatha patted his hand. "My dear boy, you want everything, all she has to offer, all she has to give, including the very next breath she breathes. Everything is your answer, now for the question. What are you willing to do to obtain it?"

Benedict swallowed, the emotion of the moment was too much for him. To see Agatha, irritating Agatha sick, to know he was making Katherine ill with heartache, and the issue with his own heart. The very heart that seemed to have trouble beating without Katherine near.

"Anything. I would do anything."

"So you'd abandon all those mistresses."

"Already done."

"You'd turn away from your devil may care attitude and vices?"

Was that even a question? "Of course!"

"And you'd give yourself fully to the one person in the world who has enough of your heart to break it. Would you do that, Benedict?"

His heart hammered in his chest. He looked from Agatha to his hands, the very same hands that all day had felt naked as if missing the other half that fit within them. "I have," he mumbled, his voice sounding foreign because of the hoarse emotion coming from his lips.

"Then what are you waiting for?"

His head snapped up. "I don't know."

With that, he jumped up from his seat and walked to the door, then on second thought, he walked back to Agatha and kissed her on the brow. "You always were my favorite aunt."

"I'm your only aunt, you rogue." She tried to laugh but instead coughed.

"And I'm so glad you are." He kissed her again and fought the emotional turmoil taking place in his heart when a single tear ran down her face.

"As am I, as am I."

He left her then, and walked down the stairs to the study where he knew he would find Baldwyn.

But the room was empty. He heard footsteps and turned.

Baldwyn had cleaned up and was ready to leave.

"Where are you going?" Benedict asked, though he had an idea.

"I have to tell her." Baldwyn was perspiring as he had been running around the house at full speed.

"Then, tell her." Benedict encouraged and laughed. "Apparently Agatha does have the final say, eh?"

Baldwyn rolled his eyes. "Do not get me started. That woman's intuition frightens me."

Both men fell silent. Then turned to look at the stairs.

"Do you think?" Baldwyn didn't finish his question.

"She said it will pass." Benedict cleared his throat. "After all, she's a tough old thing. It isn't as if she is doing to die."

Baldwyn nodded his head. "You're right. Paranoia is a side effect of too much drinking I hear."

At that, Benedict laughed and walked out of the house, in search of one woman that could bring him to his knees.

Chapter Twenty-three

How Much Do I Love Thee?

Katherine hated to admit that every time there was a noise, she ran to the windows and plastered her face against the glass hoping in vain that it would be Benedict's curricle outside, meaning he had come to call again.

After rejecting him again this morning when all the lovely books arrived, she hadn't the heart to do it again.

Granted, she was hurt, upset, and at the most ridiculous moments felt that she would burst into tears.

Could she trust him with her heart? He had said as much. He had promised they would marry and be happy.

But he hadn't promised fidelity. Nor had he fully explained his situations with the many mistresses.

Then again, it was natural that he would have done some horrendous things a gentle bred lady wouldn't hear about. After all, he didn't just obtain his nickname from all his many scandals and running around his house in the nude.

The question that burned at the back of her mind was,

what if? What if he was to change? What if he wanted to change? What if he was trying?

Yet, it seemed so foolish. Surely every girl thought such things when wanting to reform a rake of the first order. Every girl wanted to be the girl that was so special she would change the devil into an angel. And she wasn't so sure she was pretty enough or exciting enough to hold his attention.

The knocker on the door announced another visitor. With great self-control she managed to sit and pretend to read one of the many novels Benedict had given her, when the door to the sitting room opened, and Benedict was announced.

She slowly put the book down. Benedict's face lit up, a smile broke out across his features, and in two strides she was in his arms, being pressed against the wall with such force she was sure her form would be permanently glued to the wallpaper. His kiss was hungry yet affectionate, as he parted her lips with his tongue and caressed her face with his hands.

Her butler cleared his throat, causing Benedict to stop, and place her once again to rights. With a few choice words, he walked to the door, shooed her butler out and turned the lock.

"I have to say something."

Katherine fumbled with her hair, averting her eyes. If she didn't look directly at him, perhaps she could be stronger and not cry.

"I'm not sorry."

Well, that was a lousy start.

She opened her mouth to speak, but he continued.

"To be sorry seems too easy. You mess up and say you're sorry, but the value of that person's apology is measured against their past indiscretions. So then you ask yourself, is that person sorry for their actions or merely sorry they had to deal with the consequences of getting caught?" Benedict laughed. "I think my entire life I've been blind. I've always felt fulfilled, never truly guilty over my actions. I boasted in my debauchery and rejoiced in the power it gave me. Until recently, I would have been merely sorry I was caught."

"And now?" Katherine asked timidly.

"Now?" He laughed bitterly. "Now I'm so blasted ashamed of myself, I want to ask the first man I see to shoot me."

"Or woman?" she volunteered.

"Yes." He laughed. "Or woman. The thing of it is I have lived selfishly from amusement to amusement, never truly realizing how hollow my existence was. Until I met you, that is, I was perfectly happy."

Great, so now she was the reason for his discontent?

"Don't take offense. I compare my prior existence to a man living in a thundercloud, until one day the clouds disappear and the most beautiful sun begins to shine light on everything. What was once acceptable in the dark, even glorified, is no longer beautiful, but ugly and distasteful. The things that seemed to be important were merely shadows, faded into my old life. I would do anything to stay in your sunlight. I would give my very soul to be your center of gravity." Benedict approached her, his trembling hand reaching out to touch her face. She closed her eyes. "So I wish to tell you, I know the true meaning of being sorry. I will not be that man, because you see, I am no longer him. I am someone new because the sun now shines. Tell me, Katherine. Tell me the sun will stay. Tell me the sun will bring light."

"I lov—"

"—Open this door immediately!" a man's voice shouted.

Benedict cursed and walked slowly to the door and unlocked it.

Paisley burst in.

"It's Agatha, we have to go, now!" Paisley grabbed Benedict and ushered him out before Katherine could finish what she was saying. Without as much of a word to anyone, she grabbed her pelisse and reticule and followed them out of the house.

She had no idea by the time they arrived they would be too late.

Nor had she quite understood the depth of anguish a man would face when his last remaining relative save his cousin, was taken from the world.

Chapter Twenty-four

One Step Forward, Two Steps Back

The funeral was depressing, as most funerals were. And Katherine was by Benedict's side the entire time holding his hand, trying to give him strength.

The worst part, he thought as he squeezed her hand, was that Agatha and he had only just begun communicating.

He looked up at the dreary London sky. Was that the life he wanted for himself? To push away everyone and everything? His last remaining family member, save his cousin, was dead.

Alone. He was alone in the world, and he had nothing to show for it really. He had no true friends to turn to. Except Katherine.

He had to tell her. She had to know before they married how he felt, what he would give away for her, what he would do for her if just given the chance. If she could not accept his love and forgive him, he may just follow Agatha into the grave, not that she would much appreciate her devilish nephew ruining her chances of happiness in the afterlife.

He laughed at the thought.

"Are you well?" she asked as they paused in front of his carriage.

"I will be, very soon." He kissed her hands. She didn't pull away but the vulnerability was visible in her gaze. "Tonight." He kissed her forehead. "At the Kringle Ball, let us dance until midnight, and when all is over with, let us marry."

"At midnight?" Katherine laughed. "For what reason?"

"Well, I do have papers making it completely legal, as well as the old vicar from our family estate staying at one of my townhomes for the holidays."

"And my parents?" Katherine asked biting her lip.

"I hope they'll attend."

She nodded slowly, and then more enthusiastically. Her father joined her side. Benedict said his goodbyes and with a final glance toward his aunt's house, jumped into his carriage.

****

Katherine readied for the ball. A pink silk ball gown of beautiful satin hung snug around her middle. The skirts fell around her legs making it impossible to see the line of the dress. It was scandalous to say the least, only because she knew Benedict would spend most of his night trying to find the outline of her legs within the folds of the fabric.

The man did have an odd obsession with her knees and ankles.

Her carriage arrived at his townhome early, but he had asked permission from her parents to escort her, especially considering they were to be married at midnight.

She was so excited, she had to clench her hands to keep from waving them wildly in the air. His speech had been so beautiful, so wonderful.

Yet part of her, a tiny part, still had doubt, for how could a man who had lived his entire life one way, hope to change in just a few weeks? And all because of her? She was nothing special, she knew that. Even Benedict had pointed it out early on in their relationship, but perhaps she should just allow herself to fall. For the only person she could imagine that she wanted to catch her was the Duke of Banbury.

She knocked. A very stunned butler opened the door and then closed it in her face. Truly, he needed to hire a new staff immediately.

She knocked again. He opened it a crack. "I'm here to see my *fiancé*. He's to be escorting me to the Kringle Ball."

"Er..." The butler looked behind him, and suddenly Katherine heard shouting. She pushed past the butler with all the strength she could muster and ran directly into her worst nightmare.

Maria, the old housekeeper wearing a gown fit for a courtesan with her chest nearly exposed, she was crying and shouting still. And then she turned to Katherine, venom in her eyes.

Benedict also turned. "This isn't what you think, she—"

"—He loves to play games, my lady. This is just one of the many ones we've dreamt up together. It makes our time together so much better when there is the fear of getting caught. We fight," she laughed, "and then we make love, right after his innocent little girl walks through the door. I couldn't write a better story myself." She tripped on the hem of her gown and laughed again.

"Katherine..." Benedict pinched his nose. "She's drunk and angry, and somehow snuck through the servants' entrance. This is no game. She is ill, sick actually, and if she steps foot in my house one more time..." Benedict reached for Maria and grabbed her arm, clenching it within his hand tightly. "I will have her arrested. Now leave before I call Bow

Street."

She jerked her arm away, tears streaming down her face. "Why would you throw away something so good?"

"We are finished!" he yelled. "You mean nothing to me. What we did, meant nothing."

"It was everything."

"Perhaps for you. For me it was nothing but a heartless toss with an easy woman who desired money in exchange for services."

Maria threw her head back and laughed, her dark hair spilling in waves across her scandalous dress. She walked past Katherine and glared. "You'll never be able to give him what I did. He'll grow tired of you and come back. Just wait and see."

With that she left.

Katherine tried to breathe, but the air wouldn't fill her lungs fast enough. Short gasps came out until finally she fell to her knees on the ground, still gasping for air.

"Katherine!" Benedict ran to her side, scooped her into his arms, and pushed open the doors to the first room on the right, one of the salons. "Katherine?"

****

Benedict had never felt so angry and afraid in his entire life. Angry at Maria, angry at himself, angry at his past, and afraid that Katherine was now lost forever. How could she trust him? How could she know that the other women meant nothing? That Maria had literally attacked him in his own home? Beating his chest until Marsail had to pull her from his body?

"Katherine?" He touched her face, then her chest. "Breathe, just breathe, in and out, slowly now. There you go, slowly."

Finally, after a few minutes her breathing slowed.

And then the tears came.

He wanted to die.

In fact, he kept eyeing the pistol hanging over the fireplace.

"Please, please don't cry." He wiped her tears, but he was too slow in catching all of them. Benedict rocked her in his arms. She was trembling.

"Nothing happened. She is mad, Katherine. Do you understand? I would never do that to you, ever. You must believe me."

She didn't say a word, merely cried a little more, then pulled herself from his lap and set her skirts to rights. "I'm ready for the ball now."

"You can't be serious?"

"I am. My parents will expect me."

He moved to grab her arm, but she pulled back. Trust was a thing of the past, if it had ever been there in the first place. And in return, he noticed the sparkle die in her eyes, and he knew he was the cause as well as the cure. She just needed time.

He patted his coat pocket to be sure he had remembered to take the note Agatha had left him. It was there. But she was not. He needed her now, needed her wisdom and guidance on how to proceed. But all he could think that she might say would be to fight. So fight he would. Wordlessly they left the house. Neither of them spoke the entire way to the Kringle Ball.

Chapter Twenty-five

The Note

Katherine had already decided to forgive Benedict. Though he did have some explaining to do, she realized one very important thing.

She didn't want to live her life in fear.

She loved him so much that she wasn't sure she could face life without him. Katherine just wanted his love in return, as well as his loyalty. The only reason she doubted him was because of what she saw with her eyes, not what she felt with her heart.

Fear had ruled her decisions with him, and she was much happier when she didn't feed it. When she allowed her trust in Benedict and in herself to make sound decisions, to lead her to happiness, fear dissipated.

So as Benedict helped her out of the carriage, she looked up at the starry sky and then back at the man she would soon call husband. She offered him something, something she was waiting to give to him at midnight tonight.

"Wait." She stopped him.

He looked miserable, as if someone had just announced the world was going to end.

"I have a gift for you."

"I-I don't need a gift," he stuttered. "Just you. I hope you understand my love for you."

Katherine stomped on his foot. Truly the nerve of the man, beating her to the punch!

"What was that for?" He cursed and began hopping.

"I was going to say that, you cad!"

"What?" He cursed again. "Apparently pain is blocking my ability to think, you were going to say what?"

"That I love you!" She threw her hands up in the air. She had wanted to say it first, to offer it to him as a gift so he knew she trusted him, wanted to belong to him. "Men!" she screamed at nobody in general, though a few women walking up the stairs began to clap.

"I'm sorry?" he offered, then backed up, no doubt afraid she would somehow wound him again.

"Well..." She crossed her arms. "I imagine it's fine. The moment's gone now."

"Can't you say it, at least for my benefit? You have nearly broken my foot."

"If I was aiming to break it, I would have."

"Oh, how true that is," Benedict muttered.

"You'll just have to make it up to me." Katherine managed a small smile and hooked her arm within his. "Let's go indoors before your toes freeze off as well."

He smiled and patted her arm. "I'm sorry about tonight, about Maria and..."

Katherine stopped walking. "Let us not speak of it again, agreed?"

"Agreed." His eyebrows furrowed, but he didn't speak. Instead he escorted her into the Kringle Ball with a confused look etched across his ducal face. Benedict's eyes narrowed, but he did not say a word.

****

Benedict hadn't spoken of the incident the entire night, but still noted the hurt he saw in Katherine's eyes. Saints alive! He wanted her trust, needed it. As well as guidance, but he had none. Nobody.

He sighed. Now was as good a time as any to read the note. It had been burning a hole in his pocket since it had been discovered. And now, as he watched Katherine weave through the crowds at the ball, the woman he had unintentionally hurt, he needed his aunt's comfort more than ever. So he walked to the corner and unfolded the letter.

Benedict, when I discovered my sickness would take me. I was bitter. I was angry. But mostly, you must understand my fear.

My two boys, the ones I helped raise, albeit with a strict hand, were going to be without me.

You, specifically Benedict, without any sort of living relative.

And I thought to myself, how can I leave him behind? How can I allow my body to deteriorate and wither away when my nephew needs so much guidance?

I have stood by and watched you make mistakes.

I have kept my mouth closed when you paraded with your mistresses.

We all have wild oats, by Jove. You'd have an apoplexy if you knew of mine.

It may have appeared that I did not approve, and perhaps according to society I didn't, but I loved you. I loved you desperately, and I have only wanted what is best for you.

I would move heaven and earth for you, my boy. For Baldwyn, too.

You see...

When your mother died, I gave her a promise. I told her you would be better than the men before you in your family, but that it would take a different strategy of sorts.

Rather than smother you, I allowed you your mistakes. Rather than coddle you, I pretended to be upset and turned my nose at your escapades. Your fear of me did not hinder my love, if anything it brought me joy, for I knew deep down that you cared, even when you claimed you didn't.

As I write this letter, I have only a few months to go on living in this world before I irritate God in His.

And I wondered, what could I possibly give Benedict? What could I leave him?

Her.

I wanted you to have her.

She reminds me of myself. She is strong, she is opinionated, she is clumsy. After all, she did try to kill you on several occasions, not a small feat, might I add.

If I leave you her, if you marry, then you will not be left alone in this world, but you will have a true family of your own. You see, my boy, we are more alike than you know. Our personalities push the limits and rejoice in the scandal and fear we bring to others. It is control, it is power, but it is not living. It is not happiness.

I want that for you.

I want you to have that love. I want you to marry her and protect her, to cherish her, to love her with a fierceness unmatched by anyone else.

This is my dying wish, my gift to you, the legacy I leave behind.

As well as half my estate…I only ask that you fill those many summer homes with the laughter of children, though I imagine you've already been working on that part behind my back, you rogue.

Remember, I love you.

Agatha

That little minx! Benedict wasn't sure whether to laugh or

cry. She knew. The woman knew the entire time. She truly had picked Katherine out for him. She'd just tricked him as he suspected. But it was a glorious trick, one for the history books no doubt, for he would fall for it all over again.

He glanced up to see Katherine approaching.

After everything they'd been through, he knew he was going to have to create one more scandal.

One more show of devotion.

So he didn't walk.

He didn't even smile.

With fierce determination, he tucked the note into his jacket pocket and ran, as fast as his legs would take him, toward her.

His family.

Gasps were heard throughout the ballroom. The music came to a halt, but he couldn't care less.

All he saw was *her*.

All he wanted was *her*.

All he needed in this world was *her*.

Unshed tears blurred his vision. His hands reached out to grasp Katherine, but touching her was not enough. With little effort, he lifted her into the air and twirled her around before crushing his lips to hers, in such a kiss that he was sure even Agatha saw the scandal from heaven.

"I love you," he said and kissed her again.

"I love *you*," she replied as tears streamed down her cheeks. Katherine wrapped her arms around him, opened her mouth to him, and kissed him so passionately he wanted to weep. As well as boast, if he was being quite honest. He remembered the Duke of Tempest causing a similar scandal a few years back.

"So," she pulled back, "the Devil Duke creates yet another scandal."

"Oh, be sure there will be many more to come." He set

her to her feet.

"Really?" She lifted an eyebrow.

"Yes, for he also plans to marry. To stay true to his wife, if she'll have him. To have loads of children, naming the first Agatha of course, because naturally she wouldn't allow us to have a boy first."

"Naturally." Katherine giggled.

"My heart...it's yours." He kissed her forehead. "It's yours forever. If you'll have it."

"Well, you did finally learn how to smile..."

He nodded.

"And, you have ruined me on numerous occasions."

His grin widened.

"Not to mention," she added, "the fact that I'm irrevocably in love with you as well."

And that was when the Devil Duke burst out laughing, causing an even greater scandal to sweep the *ton*, for it was the first time anyone ever heard him laugh.

"Christmas miracle?" people whispered amongst themselves.

But Benedict didn't care. He had his love, his life, his family, and he had his aunt to thank for that. God bless her. She had given him the best gift of all.

The gift of family.

Epilogue

Three years later.

"Agatha!" Benedict screamed. They were going to be late for the Kringle Ball, and his daughter of two was currently running through the house naked.

Like father, like daughter he supposed.

His valet still hadn't quit, but he knew one day he would lose his mind. If anything, Benedict's own nakedness had become worse what with having a wife around all the time.

Clothes? Who needed clothes?

His valet did not agree.

Nor did his butler, but he gave them enough bonuses every Christmas not to care, so he figured he was safe.

"Agatha," he said quietly when she approached him giggling. "You need to go upstairs with Nanna. Mother and I are leaving for the night. Can you do that for us?"

She shook her head no.

Of course.

He swore up and down that Agatha, while in heaven, chatted up God and told him how amusing it would be to gift them with a child who took exactly after both their parents, to a fault.

And God, being in good humor and loving Agatha as he should, granted her this one boon.

Little Agatha smiled up at him and giggled again, his heart thumped with joy. "You must get some clothes on before Mother sees you."

"Before I see what exactly?" Katherine floated down the stairs looking every inch the duchess, and every inch the seductress. Heavens how he loved her. It seemed the longer they were married the more their love grew, until most days he felt so stupidly happy that he couldn't wipe the smile off his face if he tried.

"Happy anniversary, love." Katherine kissed him on the cheek then looked down. "Agatha, sweetheart, why aren't you wearing clothes?"

"Papa!" Agatha squealed. "No clothes too!"

Katherine glared at Benedict. He winked shamelessly and then she blushed from the roots of her hair down her glorious neck. He leaned forward to take a peek down her dress.

She pushed him away. "Those are the very things you should not be doing in front of your daughter. She already copies everything else."

They both looked down at their grinning little girl and laughed.

Nanna came rushing down the stairs and scooped up Agatha, scolding her for running away during bath time.

"She takes after you," Katherine said.

"Does not."

"Does too! She runs around naked and ignores anyone's pleas to do otherwise!"

"She also tried to kill me three times. So who exactly does she take after in that regard?"

"It was four," Katherine argued. "And she didn't try to

kill you. They were all accidents. It wasn't her fault you fell into the pond while taking her for a walk, or out of the tree when getting her an apple. You just need to be more careful."

Benedict grimaced, *careful* and his daughter were not anywhere near the same thing. The more he coddled her, the more it seemed she wanted to do something daring.

Unfortunately, it reminded him of himself, which frightened him more than words could express.

Luckily, he had Katherine.

And with her, he could do anything.

"Why are you smiling?" Katherine put her hands on her hips, tilting her head.

"Why shouldn't I be smiling?" His grin grew.

"You look like you're about to do something…"

He grabbed her hands and ran into the study, shoving the door closed behind them and with little effort lifted her skirts.

"Benedict!" she scolded. "What are you doing! We're going to be late!"

"Then we'll be late. I am a duke after all."

His argument to get away with anything.

She rolled her eyes and squirmed happily beneath his touch. "But it's our anniversary and everyone is going to want to see us. Oh!" She leaned in and kissed him. "Maybe just this once.

"That's my girl." He kissed her firmly across the mouth.

And an hour later, when they arrived at the ball hand in hand, Benedict's past reputation was merely a shadow on everyone's lips. Had he really been all that bad? People wanted to know. For what they saw now was a man completely changed from the one he was before.

And it was all because his aunt loved him enough to trick him. God rest her soul.

About the Author

Rachel Van Dyken is the USA Today Bestselling author of regency and contemporary romances. When she's not writing you can find her drinking coffee at Starbucks and plotting her next book while watching The Bachelor.

She keeps her home in Idaho with her husband and their snoring Boxer, Sir Winston Churchill. She loves to hear from readers! You can follow her writing journey at www.rachelvandyken.com.

Also by Rachel Van Dyken:

The Ugly Duckling Debutante
The Seduction of Sebastian St. James
The Redemption of Lord Rawlings
Every Girl Does it
The Parting Gift
Waltzing With the Wallflower
Savage Winter
Upon A Midnight Dream
Whispered Music
Beguiling Bridget
Compromising Kessen

Astraea Press

Pure. Fiction.

www.astraeapress.com

CPSIA information can be obtained at www.ICGtesting.com
Printed in the USA
LVOW06s2152220414

382840LV00004B/329/P